D1527719

THE DROWNED LIBRARY

PAUL KERSCHEN was born in 1978 and grew up in Tucson. He received an MFA from the Iowa Writers' Workshop and a Ph.D. from the University of California-Berkeley, and has won the Iowa Arts Fellowship and Glenn Schaeffer Fellowship. He lives in California.

Best wishes—

1.12.2012

THE DROWNED LIBRARY

PAUL KERSCHEN

FOXHEAD BOOKS

Portland | Tipp City

The Drowned Library. ©2011 by Paul Kerschen. All rights reserved. Printed in the United States of America. No part of this book may be used or reproduced in any manner whatsoever without written permission except in the case of brief quotations embodied in critical articles and reviews. For information, address Potemkin Media Omnibus, Ltd., 8 S. 3rd St. Tipp City, OH 45371.

Library of Congress Data
Kerschen, Paul
    The Drowned Library / Paul Kerschen.—1st. ed.
        135p. 23cm.
ISBN-13: 139780615492988
ISBN-10: 100615492983
    1. Fiction—Literary. 2. Fiction—Short Stories

For Jessie, as they are

Großer Bär, komm herab zottige Nacht

ATLAS

You go to the war because you're poor. You start out poor and you'll go to the war. All your family in the world is a sister and Uncle Sam, and it's your uncle who has your back. He's the doctor at Fort Benning who puts you on double rations because you're built, he says, like a mosquito hawk, and he's the D.I. who smokes you all night, hanging water jugs off your wrists, because that morning you fell out of line to use the head. The smoking takes you up against a wall in yourself, a limit of exhaustion, without breaking you apart—and later, once you get your arms back, you feel joy. You just learned to keep yourself. Then basic training is done with and you're overseas, sprinting through the dark and bleeding in the sand, and then your tour is done with and you're back home in El Paso, because no other city remembers your name in its nighttime prayers, out with your sister and her husband at Arturo's, because what else is there to do in the dark, drinking Bud and scratching your forearms under the counter and thinking about shooting pool if the college kids ever get off the table, because you're home now and your uncle is done with you.

Brent, your sister's husband, is old enough to be your uncle. He takes up the stool next to you and leans his corduroy sleeves on the bar and tells his beer about the country. It's the only thing that ever listens to him, that mug of Bud Light, but he'll talk as long as it's there. If you tune in you'll hear things like, "a plan, a systematic plan to distract the electorate with, with non-issues, so as to keep them voting against their own actual economic interest"—and then you tune back out. The kids who take his writing class at UTEP must bite their lips bloody trying to keep awake.

Liz sits next to him in her dark eyeliner, in her heap of dark bangs. Okay, Brent, she'll say, or who do you mean, Brent, or how do you know that, Brent. She must have more to say—you remember her as a talker—but Brent doesn't leave anyone else much talking room. His mouth seems to have been open as long as you've known him, with the same word always falling out and bouncing off the air and falling out again. When you left for Fort Benning he was just your sister's old writing teacher who'd started hanging around her in the evenings; now you're home and he's married to your sister and he still has the same word in his mouth. It was your first thought, that afternoon you brought your bags to their door and he took you back to the bed you'd be sleeping in—you thought, the guy doesn't move through time.

"You have to think critically," he tells you. "You have to see past the slogans." With you his voice always takes on a pleading edge, because you won't agree with him, and you won't argue with him. He wasn't there. Easy to disbelieve in America when you've never been out of it.

"Just their vocabulary ought to clue you in. They want you to believe it's a war like, that this is World War Two. And it can't be. We aren't fighting an enemy state."

"He knows who we're fighting, Brent," says Liz. "He don't need a lesson on it."

"Perspective, hon," he says, "this is critical perspective," and gives you a jolly smile, this fattish goateed teacher who beds down with your sister every night and wants to be your friend. Liz sips her cranberry juice and drops her hand to the bulge where your nephew or niece is growing, and the three of you turn quiet and listen to the oil of time oozing past. By the calendar you've been home three months, but these nights all have a way of becoming the same night, the same four or five beers' worth of dark hours at Arturo's, getting talked at by Brent, watching the TV's underwater flicker on Liz's face, wanting to go shoot pool but not getting up because you'd rather keep a wall at your back. It all reminds you of something Holmes once said—that time will never end but the world can only take so many shapes, so you have to be sure of everything you do because it'll come back again and again forever. Of course Holmes might have been kidding. But maybe it's true even so, that this is eternity and no one knows it. No heaven, no hell, just Arturo's.

"You got another interview tomorrow?" Liz asks.

"Where's it at?" says Brent. "The construction outfit? I mean, I'm sure that would be fine, but I was going to say that just today I talked to my friend at the advising center. I told her how you're good with numbers and everything, and she'd love to have you in for a talk. Just to float some classes. Because I did a bit of research too, actually, on the Army tuition program, and they'll cover up to two-fifty a credit. That's math you can do, right? Because as far as living expenses, Liz and I don't want you to worry for now." He grins as always, wanting you to pick up his half-jokes. He thinks it's a kindness to remind you how every bite you eat and every minute you sleep is on his dime.

"Being where you are," he says, "I think you have an opportunity—"

"Let him do what he wants," says Liz.

"Sure," he says, too quick, and drops his head. "Time for another round?"

He goes over to the tattooed bar girl and waves his heavy arm at the tap, and you think of Holmes. One of the thousand things Holmes could do that you can't was to hold up an argument. His words wouldn't always make sense afterward, when you thought them over, but in his mouth they sounded certain. He seemed to be speaking your own soul.

"I didn't mean no pressure about the interview," says Liz. "You can stay with us as long as you need. You know that."

Liz with her powdered skin and plump cheeks, her soft drooping eyes: all you've got in the world. No, that isn't true. You have a working twenty-two-year-old body, a G.E.D. and a service record and a head for numbers. So where's the glue to hold it together?

"Brent don't mind neither. I promise. He wants to see you on your feet."

Brent jokes with the bar girl while the pitcher fills up. He didn't start out poor, and he didn't go to the war. He went to school up north somewhere, came out to teach in El Paso, found a cheap duplex and a wife with a steady hairdresser's paycheck and set himself up a home. It's all big cluttered rooms in their place, too dim even with the lights on, all shelves and creased-up paperbacks. Ever since you were a kid you've had trouble reading. Your eyes don't grab the letters somehow, the words jump around the page and don't turn into sounds. So it's depressing to sit by yourself around these hundreds of books that Brent must have read back in his twenties, and most of the time you end up in a corner of the living room, keeping quiet while he reads the Internet and listens to National Public Radio and gets more and more exercised about the people who are driving the USA off a cliff. And he really does care about the USA. He cares about a lot of things. He just doesn't know about the heat, how the sun washes the color out of the sky and dust gets up your nose. Right when you sneeze there's a crack and a jolt, and for a second you're confused because the jolt seemed like part of the sneeze, and then you look off to the side because you thought Holmes was pointing to something. But Holmes isn't moving. His clear eyes are aimed at you and his lips are parted a little, about to speak, and the mess under his chin is bright and wet. You grab his hand, hard and warm, a person's hand, and he still smells like a person, old sweaty Holmes on the hot road, looking and not looking at you like he's about to crawl out of his own frozen skin. The guys in the back seat are standing up and grabbing for the wheel, and someone's laying down fire—but who's the enemy, which of those outlines is the enemy, on the road, beside the road, in the doorways, cutting off Brent at the bar. You jump off your stool, grabbing at your ankle, and find your balance crouched on the floor. Then you rise slow, with a hot face. The two Mexicans at the bar give you flat looks, pull at the brims of their caps and turn away.

And here's Brent with the pitcher. "Hey," he says, "did something—?"

You'll handle him in a minute. You need to go to the bathroom. And the bathroom is another pain in the ass because of another stupid coincidence, like the forever stupid coincidence of Mexicans looking like Iraqis and the desert here looking like the desert over there. The problem is, you have to do your business without turning the light on, because over the urinal there's a sign you don't want to see. It advertises an Atlas Gym, not a local place, with a drawing of a kneeling muscleman, head down and the world on his shoulders. When you were a kid, at school or church or one of the foster homes, you had a book of maps with that same figure on the back. You mentioned it once to Holmes, after you'd been out humping your packs all day, and he laughed and told you everything you'd never known: that Atlas was a prisoner in ancient times, that he'd fought the holy gods and been given that job as punishment. For the sweaty two of you, with shoulders rubbed raw and grit in your eyes, it made a lot of sense.

"Because what keeps us out here?" Holmes asks. "Why are we fighting?" When you don't answer he lifts his fingers and says, "Code of Conduct training—love of and faith in our country. A conviction that our cause is just. Belief in our democratic institutions and concepts. Right? So the question is, how does that get us out to the sandy asshole of the world? And you know how. The enemy took it to us, so we have to take it to the enemy. We fight them here, lest we fight them at home. Because this out here—" He spreads his fingers over the palm trees, the jumbled white roofs and colorless sky. "This is the absolute edge of the world. Just like for Atlas. They had him out on the rock of Gibraltar, the edge of the Mediterranean, which was the edge of the world in those days. That's where he held the sky up. Because otherwise it would come down on the folks at home."

Holmes did more reading than anyone you knew. Socrates and Zarathustra, the life of Jesus, Egyptian pyramid power and the Chinese art of war. There was always a battered volume or two in his pack—no joke, on a long day of patrol, to load an extra pound in your pack—and any spare moment he'd pull it out, flip it open while he lit his cigarette, read favorite parts aloud. He never stopped trying to lend them to you, though he knew what a slog it was for you to read through anything. He was tough. He wanted to break your barriers.

Remembering this, you've pulled a small can of lighter fluid from inside your jacket and shaken it cold against your palm. On its own the fluid makes you sick, just like drinking makes you sick, but together the two seem to balance out. When you spray your nostrils and breathe in, the beer, which had been huddling your brain like wet cloth, lifts with magical speed and makes you into a weightless shower of sparks, a huge smile zooming up like a pair of bat wings. After a second it dips down and you spray again and zoom again, not quite as high this time, until you end up perched on a ledge with all your edges tingling and a red-blue grid in your eyes like a broken video screen. Sometimes your dreams are like this. And even your dreams the Army wanted into; they asked about nightmares on the post-deployment sheet, the one where you marked everything "no." To wake in the dark, broken up and not knowing where you are, isn't the same as having nightmares. Because you know how those people end up.

Tucking away the can, you feel like forgiving the world. Is it the Mexicans' fault they look like Iraqis? Doesn't most of the world look that way? Same inky hair, same toasted skin, just the eyes and noses pushed or pulled one way or the other. Even the mustaches—all over the world, any country you like, everyone's growing Saddam mustaches. You giggle, picturing Brent with a Saddam mustache, Liz with a Saddam mustache, their unborn kid with a Saddam mustache, press together your buzzing lips and spurt out another laugh—yes, you're feeling worlds better. In fact you could stand to turn the light on. You step back to the door, soles sticking a bit in the floor muck, and feel for the switch. The fluorescent rod flashes once, twice, then holds steady over the mirror, the urinal with its pink cake, the Atlas sign with its kneeling muscleman, Holmes kneeling in the same pose next to the urinal. For a second he keeps still, head down and arms up around an imaginary globe, then lifts his head and grins at you.

"Thought you were never going to turn it on."

You grin right back. Your smile is for the whole world, but above all for him. He cocks his head at the Atlas sign.

"Didn't forget our pal here, did you?"

It's a joke. It's all an old Holmes joke. He drops his arms and you reach to help him up. He looks just as you remember: olive-skinned with heavy cheeks and brows, geared up for patrol in his helmet and field jacket, the flak vest bulking up his ribs. When you hug him he's warm and solid as a man ever was.

"No kisses now, you fag." There's the same quickness in his lips and eyes, the same half-checked mocking spirit. Someone bangs on the door and you freeze, ashamed, but Holmes pushes on past and opens up. The guy outside smirks at the two of you—you can hear the joke he wants to make—but Holmes stands tall in his body armor and makes a terrible face, bunching down his eyebrows like a Halloween mask, until the guy drops back, quelled. You march outside. In the dim light you can just make out a flesh-colored bandage on Holmes's throat, covering a good patch of skin but well camouflaged. It's not something anyone else would notice.

How are you going to sit him down with Liz and Brent? But he understands everything; he goes right up, shining welcome out of his face like a big brown sun, and introduces himself as your war buddy Specialist Holmes. Brent shrinks a little behind his goatee and you have to smirk; you've wanted to see that for a long time. But then he collects himself and stands, shakes Holmes's hand and says it's a real honor. Can he buy Holmes a beer?

"I would let you do that, Brent. That'd be right kind."

Brent goes off. Holmes makes small talk with Liz, asking the simple questions—what do you do for a living, how's El Paso suit you, when's the baby due. After a minute she drops her surprise and starts telling him things you didn't even know, that she isn't planning to work her whole life at the hair salon, that once the baby's old enough she wants to start night classes and finish her associate's degree. What she really wants is to get the hell out of Texas and move to San Diego. When she closes her eyes at night she sees palm trees, ocean waves. Her cheeks draw in, her eyes turn bright and she looks suddenly beautiful, which isn't how you usually see your sister. You understand it's Holmes making it happen. She's reaching into herself and bringing out this beauty because Holmes is making her love him, just like he made you love him. And here's Brent with his beer.

"You don't know what it means," says Brent, "to meet one of our boy's comrades in arms. The stories you must have."

"Ah, stories," says Holmes. "Well, he was great over there."

"We know he's great," says beautiful Liz.

"But do you really?" asks Holmes. "Because I think you look at him and say, here's the kid who's staying with us. A young man now but still kind of a kid, not too smart, not too dumb, doesn't cause trouble around the house but needs to start pulling his weight forty hours a week like everyone else. Am I right?"

"Well, I don't think that's fair," says Brent. "We don't begrudge him a place to sleep."

"And I respect your not begrudging, but that's not the same as being glad. You can love somebody and still think, in the end he weighs so many pounds and when's he going to start pulling them. But listen." Holmes drops his voice. "You don't know what he did over there.

Ever hear of a place called Abu Amri? Well, you wouldn't. It's a little village that never got in the news because it never had a scandal. Just plain everyday fighting and dying. One summer morning your boy is driving a Humvee into Abu Amri—one of our shit Humvees with no armor, that we had to armor ourselves with sandbags and scrap metal pulled off Iraqi tanks. We called it the cardboard coffin. And the cardboard coffin tripped an IED." Holmes folds his hands and sweeps his eyes around. "Now you can ask a hundred times what happened next, and you'll get a hundred different answers. In combat you don't have a map, you don't know where anything is except the spots on your body where you might get hit, and all you can do is try to keep those spots in front of you and not behind you. One man was killed right away in the Humvee—shrapnel through the neck. And maybe the Humvee was still in driving shape, maybe not, maybe it was on fire, but anyhow your boy finds himself out of the vehicle, against a wall with a firefight on. Thirty yards past a stretch of weeds is a little square window, and death is coming out from inside it. Flash and bang, hold off, flash and bang again. Dirt flying everywhere. The sergeant's yelling that we can't engage, there's no air support, everyone fall back in the Rhino Runner and drive out. But what does your boy see in the weeds?"

Holmes raises his eyebrows at Liz and Brent, and for a moment you think they might answer. "What he sees out there is an Iraqi family. A man and wife and child. They're crouched down in the dirt, too scared to move, and the kid is huddled up between her parents but even so your boy can see she's been hit. There's blood all over her hands and clothes. He doesn't think. Because if he was thinking he would move the hell out, run back along the wall firing bursts at the window and load himself safe in the Rhino. But what does he do instead?" Holmes nods. "Yeah. He drops his rifle loose in the sling and runs into the weeds. He grabs the kid from her father just yards from that window, then turns around and runs back, not lifting his head and not firing a shot, just carrying the kid on a steady course back to the Rhino. And she turned out to have a punctured lung. Getting her to the field hospital saved her life."

Holmes bows his head and turns up his palms, as if presenting your soul. Liz stares at him, then gives you a look like you haven't seen since you came home. "We never heard," she says. "He's a hero."

"I—wow," says Brent. "How could you never tell us?"

"He's modest," says Liz. "Look, he's embarrassed."

"He's like Atlas," says Holmes. "Old Atlas carrying us all on his shoulders and never saying a word."

"Now don't leave yourself out," says Liz. "You must have carried your share."

"Well," Holmes laughs, "I'm not here to praise myself. I did my job like anyone."

And how unspeakably generous of Holmes, to say all this for you and not a word for himself when he was the real hero, when he was lying dead in the Humvee that whole time. It's almost awful to get so much love. But Holmes has a message for you in his eyes, and that message is: go ahead and take it. Be strong and take what's yours. And it comes to you that you don't hate Brent, that Brent is honorable, and you don't pity Liz, she has more strength in her than you ever imagined, and it's no shame or hardship to live beside them, there's a place in El Paso even for you.

"It's funny about Atlas," Brent says then. "If you mean the mythological figure. Because it's a misconception, actually, that he holds up the earth."

"Is that so?" says Holmes.

"He holds up the heavens," says Brent. "You're probably thinking of the famous sculpture in Naples, which I was lucky enough to see once—and he is holding up a sphere, but it's the celestial sphere, you know. With constellations."

"Well," Holmes says, "who ever would have thought." Then he jogs you with his elbow. "Hey, you got your huffer out here?"

But he shouldn't ask that now. Not in front of everyone.

"What, you ashamed?" He leans into you, not quite angry, just wanting to remind you that he can do as he likes. So you reach in your jacket and hand over the can. Liz and Brent peer a little as he shakes it up, trying to figure out what it is, and Liz gives you a shocked look just as he opens his mouth and sprays in. He shuts his eyes, giggling low, then opens them to show wide pupils dancing with light.

"A big job for a big man," he declares in a sepulchral voice. The cold spray ices up the voice box for a second. You look around the bar to see if anyone has their eye on you, but it's just the usual college kids and ball-capped Mexicans, the TV's aquarium shimmer and time clutching it all, catching everything in its gears and ratcheting it back over and over.

"Well, I teach writing at the university," Brent says. "To a lot of returning soldiers. We'll do exercises where they write out their memories—"

"Oh, memories," says Holmes, "if it's memories you want, I can go all night." No one answers. "Let's talk about the cities," he suggests. "Let's talk about the fucked-up police work you have to do in the cities. Because any of those trucks could have a bomb in it, any of those women could be dynamited up under her robe, and how are you going to check them all? Every family's allowed one AK-47 in the home. More than that and dad's coming back to the base. And it's not like these people are in a real army, they're a bunch of bus drivers and shish kebabbers who got talked into their bullshit uprising, so you can't even call them POWs. They're persons under captivity. And the only consolation in being a fucked-up policeman is that no one wrote any rules for persons under captivity. So you can do what you want.

"But Christ!" he shouts, slapping the bar. "All they want is to cut each other to bits. It's not a city, it's a rat trap with a thousand walls. And walls mean nothing over there, the goddamn ten-foot concrete barriers disappear when they smash a truck in. So this is no help." He bangs on his helmet. "And this is no help." He slaps the flak vest. "Only if they'd give you night goggles. I mean real night goggles. Because walls don't mean anything, and trucks don't mean anything and people don't mean anything, they're just how the bombs move, and you need some goggles that would peel off the appearances and show the naked bombs. Get it? The cell phone wired to a ball of nails. The dynamite belt coming up the sidewalk. The truth of things."

He's been loosening the helmet and vest as he talks, and now he shakes them off along with the field jacket, changing his shape. Under the gray tank top you see his natural bulk, the muscles climbing his arms and shoulders and holding up his square head like a mounted cannon. He drops his gear on the floor, loud, and people glance your way.

"So let's talk truth," he says, stretching his arms. "Because the truth is, after you've been out there all day you want to unload, and with no drink per General Order Number One and no pussy per General Order Number One and the base full of other people's pucs who don't speak English, and you don't know what they're in for but for all you know they were setting up RPGs on the corner—well, you start things. Just smoke them a bit, like we all got smoked in training. Tie rags over their eyes, put them in stress positions. Hang water jugs off their wrists. Strip them—" He halts as if ashamed, but his face is set in anger. "You know how it works. Ben looks at Darryl to see if it's okay and Darryl looks at Mike to see if it's okay, and no one's around to say it's not okay, but everyone knows Command wants them demoralized when intel shows up. So we get a couple of them stripped and cuffed in the holding cell, scrawny fucks starved on flatbread their whole lives, with sad little dicks hanging down like bits of yarn. Someone's talking like they're Ken dolls, make Mohammed Ken marry Osama Ken, and in the middle of this a squad comes back from patrol with a kid who's new to the unit. Texas boy, in fact. We called him the Queer Steer, though who knew what he actually was. He just had the look, freckles and eyelashes and big lips and all. So the Queer Steer's in the next room trying to put away his gear and we're laughing and calling him to come in, we got a couple of boyfriends for you, and his face gets pink and he kind of shakes his head without looking up. It's funny, soon as a guy shakes his head without looking up, you know you can do anything. So we grab him by the shoulders and pull him in, yelling the Manwich sandwich, it's time for the Manwich sandwich, and the Queer Steer's shouting for us to let go, kind of squirming and trying to get an arm loose, which just makes it funnier since any of us could hold him back with one hand, and we all circle around him, almost pushing him on top of the pucs, and the pink drains out of his face. We all get quiet. The pucs have been quiet the whole time, except the one on the bottom is whimpering a little. You'd think they would holler in their language or something, but all they do is whimper. The Queer Steer stares at us, stares down at those skinny backs and asses with nasty curls all over them, and finally he says—I don't go for this. Fuck you if you think I go for this. So he pulls back his boot and kicks the top puc in the ribs. And we all take turns. Finally we turned out the lights and beat on them with chem sticks until the plastic broke and spilled the glow-in-the-dark yellow shit all over them. That was funny as hell, seeing them glow, but next morning they had burns all over. They were curled up on the cement with their backs blistered up, not moving a muscle. And then intel came and got them."

For a while Brent's been opening his mouth in the goatee and shutting it again. Holmes reaches for his mug and downs the whole thing in a long swallow. "But that Texas boy," he says, wiping his mouth, "on my honor we never called him the Queer Steer again. Matter of fact, he and I got to be friends. We'd go on patrol together—" His head falls into a reminiscent shake; then he pulls up the wicked grin and leans forward. "So who do you think that boy was?"

Brent doesn't answer. He and Liz look like they'll never speak a word again. Above the bar are some Christmas lights strung over a cow skull, blinking left and then right, and to follow that sequence, to think how it spins itself eternally out, makes you want to shut your eyes for good. You shift your left ankle. About the hunting knife you carry there you feel like you feel about the huffer; sometimes it gives you comfort, sometimes you're ashamed that you can't leave it at home. But this is the world you have to get through. Finally Brent draws breath and speaks.

"I think it's time for you to go home," he says.

"You don't like my story?" asks Holmes.

"I think it's time for you to finish your beer and go home. I don't know if you're making things up, and I don't really care. I'm done talking with you."

"Well." Holmes lifts his brows, looks at Liz, looks at you. "Pardon me for giving you some news. Pardon me for thinking you'd be *curious*—" he straightens on his stool— "about what it's like when you're out holding up the goddamn world."

"Not the world I know," says Brent. "And not the boy I know. I don't care what you tell me. He's home now."

What's happened to Brent? Where's the fattish teacher whose face you couldn't stand? It's like you're seeing him in X-ray, with his inner outline shining through the heavy face and dumpy clothes and revealing what you'd never have guessed, that he's a man. His sheltering arm is stretched in front of Liz, still beautiful as you've never seen her, and it seems you must have been wrong about Holmes's purpose. You thought he was coming out as a voice to speak the truths you couldn't. But maybe he's more like an X-ray light, and maybe the things he shows you would never have seen on your own.

"You might be home," says Holmes. "But your boy isn't. You don't get this, that you can look straight at somebody and not have a clue where his world is." He lifts a hand and lets it linger at his throat, brushing the bandage. "They told us we were all together out there, but that's a lie. Everyone holds up his own world. And that's the funny thing. Because if you're holding it up, what's holding you up? Why doesn't everything fall down together?"

Brent draws his arm tighter over Liz. Is that a real question? Is it a question you asked yourself as a child, tormented by the map book with its unreadable names?

"All you can do is hold it *together*. Look!" Holmes lifts his arms around the imaginary globe. "He's not holding it up, he's holding it together. Because it wants to come apart. If he lets go, everything goes."

Slowly Holmes brings his arms down, pulls the left in close even as the right keeps moving, reaches under his pant cuff and comes out balancing the bright lines of your hunting knife. Brent goes stiff, pushes Liz behind him and sends his free arm roaming over the counter until he finds a glass mug. That's all? Not even a bottle to break? People have been looking your way more and more and now someone calls out—seeing the knife glitter, surely, under the Christmas lights and the TV screen—and all the talk in Arturo's cuts out like an unplugged stereo, leaving only the murmuring television and a few whispers that won't come into the open because Holmes is looking around the room with the knife in plain view, challenging it to rise against him. Slowly he gets to his feet, straightens his body and spreads his great arms.

"Just me holding it together," he calls to the room, hefting the blade with little gestures, tossing and dropping the point. "My world over there, my world over here."

And you know he's right. He could stick his hand right through the bar if he wanted. He could wish away the tables and chairs, the lights and people, your own watching eyes, all with a word.

"No," Liz says.

Holmes swings his head around and aims it down at her, at brave Liz with both hands on Brent's shoulder. "You never knew my brother," she says. "Someone with his face, maybe. Someone with his eyes and his name. But not the boy I know."

Up go the corners of Holmes's quick lips, into a tight agony of a smile. It's funny to him, hellishly funny that she would try this defense. And he'll answer with the knife. You see his giant's height looming over the bar, his frozen muscles bunched out with the world's weight, about to lift the blade and not lifting it. Why not? The Christmas lights blink over his body, back and forth, and right then you understand something about time in El Paso. You thought it was Brent who wasn't moving. You thought time stopped around him. But your angle was wrong. Everything's moving, everything's always moved except for Holmes and except for you. He can't touch Liz and Brent because they're already gone from here.

A thirst breaks loose in your throat and fills your eyes—who knows how long it's been caught there. Now you know: Liz and Brent are out in America, moving on through time, and you're still underneath in America's shadow. Your tears break the bar into a wash of shapes, words too blurry to read. Let them go. You sniff and dust fills your head, you stand and feel the old sun around you. It's a long time you've wanted to be back in the clean sand with no questions. Your heart thumps madly, but your movements are sure; you creep up to where Holmes sits crouched, with both his palms up and the knife resting across them. Poor Holmes, with all that muscle and nowhere to turn it.

"Can't I let it go?" he asks the knife. "If it's only my world?"

You take him in an embrace, warm and solid as a man ever was. His big hands give up the knife, and he waits dumbly for you to find his throat and begin cutting the bandage away. It's stuck tight and the job takes a while before you can let him drop. The bright wet covers his throat just as you remember, but he's no longer about to speak. He was wrong about the world. Once you've lifted it up you can't let go. It's no longer yours to put down. That's how simple it is, simple as carrying that child out of the firefight, and knowing it earlier would have saved you a lot of heartache. But nothing will be lost now. When your flesh is gone you'll hold it up with your bones. Your heart is still thumping madly, trying to get out of you, and you swing the knife inward and set it free.

ELEAZAR

It might all have gone differently, if it hadn't come in such a bad year. There are people who will lay out money for their souls even when they can't afford two palms of wheat for supper, but we never had that sort in Bethania. I was a luxury to them; I only came to their minds in autumn, after the olive harvest, if it had been a good harvest, and that summer there had been freak storms bringing a hideous new bug to the trees, black and wriggly with wavy antennae and bright red spots that turned into a bright red smear when you crushed it. Its worms burrowed through the olive pits. The other afflictions followed: new taxes, police, bunk coins, mildew in the grain. Just before the equinox a neighbor of mine was caught out after curfew and had his calf tendons slit. What I mean to say is that no one was looking out for any work of the soul, benign or malign, and I had nothing to do but stay home with the fusty papyri I'd had copied in Alexandria, back when I had money to throw around, and eat my twice-daily lentils and bread. Short on honey, short on tallow. No perfume in the oil. Then in the first parch of spring Marta came up the hill, Marta whom I'd once cared for very much, and told me that her brother was dying.

Of course I was sorry to hear it. Even if Eleazar only took me as an amusement nowadays, we'd once been friends. But after they had decided that a rogue Sadducee, or whatever they thought I was, wouldn't be marrying into the family, they stopped calling on me except for occasional services that might well have been jokes. I was invited once into their beautiful hewn-stone washroom for an exorcism, though surely no one believed there was a demon in the washroom. I've often doubted my work—I've often doubted there's a solitary real demon to be found in the Levant—but we require our daily bread. So I went ahead and lit the candles and shouted in the tongues of power until everyone seemed satisfied that the demon was gone; and Eleazar paid me half again the usual fee.

I brought Marta a cup of water and asked what had taken her brother. The hill fever, she said. Hill fever! These people had no method for naming their illnesses; she might mean any odd heap of symptoms. Not for the first time, I wished I'd studied Greek medicine in Alexandria. I might have done some good.

"Maryam's dancing over him," she added.

"Dancing?"

"Like the Galileans. She thinks it will help."

All I knew was that it was hopeless. Whatever had knocked askew the balance in Eleazar's body, its principles of dampness and heat, no dance would set it right.

"Well, does he want a blessing?" I asked. "The usual fee?"

"We thought you'd want to see him."

Her hard voice surprised me. I hadn't thought anyone in that family still cared about me enough to get angry. Marta had kept her youth, with a bit of dark paint around her eyes, strong calves under her skirts, dust on her bare feet; she had better hurry, I thought, and take up with a man before she got too old. I collected my things and followed her shifting hips down the hill, into the shade of the olive plot fronting their house. It was the long white middle of the day, the sleepy hour of locust buzz and hot wind in the leaves. Thrushes hopped in the dust and poked at bits of bark. Their family had the best home in the village, built Roman style with quicklime on the walls and a square doorway opening to a courtyard. Inner doors gave onto the beautiful things in their rooms: cedar tables, dining couches, cloths and mirrors and beads and all the rest. I half expected the whole thing to be some new joke, but as we came to a back room I caught a terrible sour smell of body. There were no windows, only a circle of candles over the earth, and I could hardly make out the pallet that Maryam was straddling. Her feet were bare but for brass hoops around her ankles; she bowed her head, swayed, shook her wrists and hair.

"Go in," Marta told me. To her sister she said, "Jesus is here."

Maryam lifted her hands and turned her kohl-lined eyes back at us. I remembered Alexandria. "Rabbi, rabbi," she chanted.

"I'm here as a friend." I squinted at the blanket between her legs. "Is he awake?"

She drew back, still in dance steps, and turned up her palms to indicate I should kneel. Where she had gotten these ideas was anyone's guess. She was susceptible, and there were always lunacies coming out of Galilee. I smoothed my frayed robe and rested my knees on the earth beside Eleazar's head. God's favor, his name meant in Hebrew, not that these people would know enough Hebrew to say if it was frogs first and blood second or the other way around. Anyhow the favors were finished now. His head was a skull wrapped in sheepskin, thrown back to expose the white throat under his beard. Far away, under his brows, the eyes wandered like stunned prisoners.

"Eleazar, old man," I said. "I've come."

His lip shook. "Water?"

Beside the pallet, on a cedar table carved in designs too lovely for the world, water pooled in a stone cup. I brought it to his lips, watched his throat clench like a fist and relax. The tip of his dark tongue ran over his mouth, and his eyes rose by degrees in their sockets until at last his spirit gazed out.

"The weeping philosopher," he whispered, and the fragment of a smile tightened his cheek. "I thought you should see."

"We never want to see suffering," I said. "I came for you."

"Did the girls hire you?"

"Only a visit."

He coughed and lifted his head. "How is it with you?" All at once he seemed no longer in the pallet, but somehow looking down from above—the old Pharisee condescension, the old Pharisee pity was still in him. Who knew what he'd heard? In the village they probably said I was living off locusts, like the prophets over the Jordan.

"I'm well," I told him.

"Truly?"

"I have my reading. For the rest, Epicurus said a pot of cheese was feast enough."

Again he made the slivered smile. "Then I can do you some good," he said. "Doesn't Epicurus tell you to meditate on death?"

"To understand it," I said. "That it's not an evil."

"Though you deny the soul?"

"Not the soul," I said.

"But you deny the next world."

"What's to pass into the next world, old man? Your soul is made of atoms like everything else. While you are, death is not. And when death is, you are no longer."

Of course he was waiting for that. His body shifted under the blanket and a thin hand emerged at his throat, clutched the wool and pulled it downward. As the blanket slid away he winced, and I smelled the waft from his body, food gone bad. Ragged strips were soaked in suppuration; in the candlelight the dark crusts seemed alive, quivering with his breath. No inch of skin was spared—only his bearded face remained whole, hanging like a separate being above the agony.

"You see, Jesus," murmured the face. "I am. And death is. I seep poison. Even to me it stinks. And you'll tell me what is and what is not? You'll deny me the next world?"

I grabbed the blanket and covered him. "I'm sorry," I said. "You don't need a lie."

Maryam still danced by the stone wall, twisting her arms above her head and shuffling her feet on the earth. Eleazar shut his eyes and a smile settled on his face, the sanctimonious look of the man who has learned to deny his senses.

"I know what I know," he said. "So can't I get a blessing from you? A denarius blessing?"

Either there was a joke in this after all, or he just wanted an obeisance from me. I waved my hand over him and muttered some Hebrew. His smile grew wider; his face nearly glowed with heat. As I stood his eyes opened and he called, as if from a great distance, "Jesus."

"Yes, old man."

"Tell me—what sort of atoms make up the soul?"

"Those most easily moved," I said. "The roundest and smoothest. Smoother than fire."

He let fly a whimpering laugh and rolled his head over the pallet. "Oh, my friend. Those books have killed you. But even for you there's life to come—" Suddenly his laugh turned into a cough, throbbing in the chest, and his sisters came to him. Maryam waved her arms; Marta knelt at his pallet, brought the water to his mouth and gave me a terrible frown.

"Go on," she said. "The purse servant will have your money."

That was unfair. She'd seen everything; she knew I hadn't meant this as a business call. But I went out to the courtyard, found the servant and told him that I'd been called in for services amounting to a silver shekel. I didn't see how anyone would begrudge it. With the bad harvests that year, you lost a denarius just in buying the day's bread and oil. After getting paid I left the house and walked out into the olive grove, where I found a group of men approaching. With the sun behind them I had trouble making out faces, but I knew these must be his friends and associates, rich Pharisees from the village. They shouldn't go up to the house just now, I told them. Eleazar was suffering, he needed rest.

"Now let me ask," I said, "if any of you have need of spiritual work. Blessings and exorcisms, divinations, lameness, sores, barren livestock—"

No one answered. Many of them wore amulets. All over Jerusalem they sold that magical junk, mostly to Temple pilgrims though locals were taken in as well: pendants, collars, bracelets, most of it not even inscribed with real language but only covered in scratches that were supposed to look like Aramaic. I suppose anyone who read Aramaic would take it for Hebrew or Egyptian. I'd never stooped to it myself. I'd come back from Alexandria expecting to teach the old Greek truths, to recover the meaning of Scripture from the false senses that had grown over its surface. But in the Jerusalem I returned to, with Hillel dead and his school out of favor, with the words of Moses forgotten—well, it was flattery and flattery until one morning you woke up in heaven. I stood a while in the olive grove, thinking this and other things, ignored by everyone. I wouldn't have chanced the prediction that Eleazar would die in that hour, not professionally, but when wailing broke out from the house I wasn't really surprised. As the crowd rushed from the grove and pressed around the door I saw Maryam and Marta step out in the day's last light, in all the beauty of mourning, their eyes turned to heaven and their linens torn to rags. Their open mouths lamented above their swells of breasts, waists like slopes of soft sand—I saw these things, and committed them to my heart's memory, while my face and throat grieved with the rest.

Wonders do happen. We have it on the authority of Scripture; further, I had worked precisely one wonder of my own, not long after coming back from Alexandria. I and some companions were walking out of Jerusalem, hungry in the afternoon, and from the road we saw the spreading crown of a fig tree. Forgetting that it was too early for figs, we climbed up to it, and when we came close enough to discover the dry buds under the leaves I was so hot and famished, so angry at our stupidity, that I cursed the plant. God must have smiled at the sheer petty evil of it. The leaves dried up as we watched, turned yellow, curled into limp insect forms and dropped from the twigs. And because this senseless thing, which I had only half intended, took place under the eyes of several reliable witnesses, I came out of it with enough reputation to begin plying a trade of blessings and curses— which should be a lesson in just how rare verifiable wonders are. Either it was the shreds of that reputation, or some more obscure sense of loyalty, that brought Maryam and Marta back to my door after a couple of days. Sometimes this happens with women, that after humiliating you to the point of death they'll decide you are joined to them by a secret and irrevocable bond.

They told me about the family matters—the binding of the limbs and jaw, the washing and anointing, the graveclothes and procession—that I hadn't attended. Too good to packed in the loose rock with the rest of us, their family had three generations of bones stacked up in a vault under the olive slopes. Of course they were somber, still in their three days' mourning, but I felt a strange excitement from them, especially Maryam who sat perfectly still on my floor with her palms clasped together and that prophetic fire in her eyes. In our youth she'd been more worldly, more like her sister, who was now recounting the burial in that flat voice we sometimes use to stave off grief. When she mentioned the blessing I raised my hands.

"I'm sorry he died so soon. But I can't take responsibility. My fees are no higher than anyone's."

"It's not that," she said. "After you left, he began to speak. Like I'd never heard."

"Like a prophet," declared Maryam.

"He said Israel will be redeemed. That the dead will walk again."

"The dead?" I'd never thought of Eleazar as having rebel sympathies—what would he have to gain, living in that beautiful house? But aspects might change at the point of death.

"And in Hebrew," said Maryam. They looked to each other, unsure. "Verabim," Marta offered. "Mish—yakit—"

It was like remembering something I had spoken myself. "*Verabim mishenei admat-afar yakitsu.* Was it that?"

Again they looked to each other. "It might be."

"Multitudes who sleep in the dust of the earth shall awake," I said. "Daniel."

"It was your blessing," Maryam said in her low voice. "It gave him God's word."

I considered it. Yes, I dared wonder if it were true. Once I had cursed by accident—might there not be an accidental blessing in the balance? I understood the danger in that thought, but it was sweet.

"You can heal him," Maryam said. "Speak the word and he'll be healed."

"Oh, no." I saw that she believed it, and for the first time I felt sad. "The dead don't wake, Maryam. It's a way of writing. What's called hyponoia—" And I actually pointed back at the papyrus rolls, as if the Stoics had something to tell her.

"For three days you don't know," she said. "It's written. The soul returns over and over to the body, trying to go back in. It only departs when the face is corrupted. A man was in the vault three days and then came out."

"Maryam," I said.

"He lived twenty-five years more. He fathered five children."

"That isn't Scripture," I told her. "It's a Pharisee story."

"It happened," she insisted.

"Where?"

"In Samaria."

I am a weak man. This was the time for me to be gentle, to send them away and let them forget that they had asked me for the impossible. But I pitied them, and no one had tried to flatter me in a long time. Marta especially was beautiful in grief; her eyes could have drowned me.

"Do you believe it?" I asked her.

"If he could really come back. You could ask anything."

Her meaning shamed us both. But she carried the shame honestly, with open eyes. "We haven't married," she said. "If our brother could walk again."

Never does the idea of providence cease to tempt us. Again and again we're persuaded that just once, this time, God has woven us a particular fate in the world, though we know by logic that He must barely remember creating it. I blushed under Marta's eyes. "You loved him so much?"

"I don't know what your quarrel was," she said. "Men have the stupidest fights over doctrine."

"It wasn't just doctrine."

"But he loved you, Jesus," she told me. "Even afterward, even at the end. I know he loved you."

I clasped my hands at my back and looked into the stack of scrolls. "It will take a little time," I said at last. "I'll need to work out the necroscopy, the thanatotropy." And I went on like that, inventing Greek words, since everyone in Bethania knew just enough Greek to say *khaire* to the legionnaires. I'm not ashamed of that part. To work as an outright fraud would have been one thing, but to think I might have real power over life and death—it frightened me. I needed faith from Marta and Maryam, even if it was only the gaping sort of faith that the illiterates placed in their gibberish amulets. I hadn't attempted a real task in so long.

We met on the hillside below the cave. These months night was not an element in itself but only a moment's absence of sun, giving the lesser lights their turn. Under the moon all the land seemed made of different shades of bone. Marta and Maryam too were beautiful bone carvings, glazed in white down to their fingernails. As we walked uphill each footstep and breath, each whine of the crickets, seemed its own significant fact. Soon the trees thinned out and we began to pass white boulders rising like ghostly sails from the grass. Each covered the mouth of a burial vault. The desert was doing its work on the wrapped corpses beneath, purging the flesh until the clean bones could be wrapped and laid in ossuaries. Best to let it vanish. I'd once been invited to an embalming in Alexandria, and to see the body's pale bags handled like holy icons under the stink of naphtha gave me terror for my future.

Marta lifted her hand to pick out Eleazar's stone; and seeing it, I felt the life drain from my legs. But I pushed forward, whispering a line of a psalm, and said to the sisters, "We'll roll it aside. Come, kneel and roll."

Under my hand the granite gave back the day's heat like a darkened bit of sun. It was broad but not deep, not meant to keep out anything larger than a jackal, and the sisters were built strong, perhaps stronger than me. Together we tore it loose from the cave mouth, sparking a rain of pebbles in the broached dark, and rolled it aside. The smell of dust masked any worse odor. Eleazar would be some distance back, and rather than crawl into the fearful place I was determined to call him out. I had spent the evening wondering how to do it, which of the old languages to use, before understanding that nothing of that sort would work. I'd never fooled him alive; I certainly wouldn't fool him dead. It would be a simple command or nothing.

"Eleazar!" I called into the hole. "Come out!"

My voice was weak. My heart prayed for silence. Crickets and wind would answer, the cave's black air would keep its own counsel, I would give the sisters my learned regrets. We would separate in walking home, each of us confirmed one degree farther in the sad old knowledge that life is life and death is death, that there is no juggling these opponents and that among all the roads leading into the grave none leads back out. To hear, then, a noise of *response* from the darkness, a shifting of rock over rock which bore to daylight sounds the same inverted relation that the fangs and bunched eyes of spiders bear to our human faces, and to hear in that shifting a kind of *speech*, as if the dead rock itself had been given a palate and tongue, as if it were made to yield a voice like a jointed carapace, the septic touch of ciliated legs, the outward tilt of reason—

"Cocksucker," it clacked. "Motherfucker."

Fear, a cold hand, rocked my spine. I felt the lightness of my body, the danger of hard stone above and below. The sisters looked to me, expecting me to comprehend it.

"Shit eater," clacked the voice. "Worm food, fly bait. Moved flesh. What do you want?"

"Who speaks?" I cried.

An ugly, clawed laugh answered. Maryam spread her arms and whispered, "Jesus, what do you hear?"

I showed her my wild face. "You don't hear it?"

"And how should they hear?" said the voice. "Who do you think is speaking?"

"Eleazar," I named it.

Again it laughed. It was a stony voice; but stone, I thought, could not be its real nature. Stone lacked soul; it had never lived, never would. Something else was speaking, that idea of rot which made death terrible, the idea of a life which, contradicting the philosophers, had ceased to be and yet persisted.

"Come out," I repeated, but my voice wavered. "Come out and walk."

"Hypocrite," it sneered. "Panderer. You've come in bad faith."

"I come in mercy."

"Mercy! You know there's only one mercy, and that is not being." *Mē einai*, it said; had we been speaking Greek all along? Maryam touched my arm and I jumped, pushing her back.

"But you are," I managed to say. "The soul speaks."

"Son of man, you don't believe your own words. How can a voice inhere in a corpse? Or is it floating above the corpse, without body? How will it move the atoms?" I stammered, and it cried, "You, *you* trying to sell life to the dead! I hope you got your fee in advance?"

My mouth flapped; my thoughts were so much wind. "You, an advocate of life?" it asked. "A beggar in rags, eating those comical lentils twice a day? What about wine, son of man? What about spices and dancing girls? Isn't pleasure the end of things?"

"We are images," I broke in, "of God—"

"Oh, now," it answered, in a register still more awful. "Are you *disputing* with me, son of man? Will you call me a third time?"

I stood dumb. I who had disputed with the subtlest tongues of Alexandria.

"If you call a third time, I will come out. And you will answer for it."

The wind turned circles in my mind. If I, a being, should encounter not-being. If not-being should irrupt into being. If it came forth—but what was it? Was it Eleazar? Had it been Eleazar?

It allowed me a while at this torture. Then it chuckled and said, "I didn't think you wanted it. Who did you think was speaking anyway? An invisible voice, that only you can hear—" And the laugh fell still lower, into thunder, an earth tremor, a blanket dropping over my mind. I reached to my side, found myself grabbing the earth and lay there with my cheek against a stone.

"Jesus—" Marta called.

A low smell, refuse or urine, drifted past. For a while I heard only the blood in my ears; then I lifted my head and saw that Marta and Maryam had begun to roll the stone back into place. Without me they could push it only in bursts, laying their hands on its surface, tensing their strong legs and shoving it a few finger-spans up the slope. The crunch of pebbles, the sighs and shifting of limbs, found a rhythm between the other rhythms of night, the crickets and my pulse. Then the grave was sealed and they turned the dim ovals of their faces back to me. I waved them off.

"When I'm stronger," I said. "Go."

Their pale shapes fell away. Far above the heavenly spheres turned their courses. Before long they would bring up the first rays of sun. I remembered the words of Heraclitus, that if the sun ever strayed from its path the Furies, ministers of justice, would set it right; and I remembered that passage in *The Canon* where Epicurus states that no sensation can be convicted of error, that even those objects presented in dreams or to madmen are true, for they cause movement in the soul, and that which is not moves not.

I lay a long time on that hill with the old words spinning in my thoughts. *To de mē on ou kinei.*

As you know, a great many things happened just after that, but I was isolated and didn't hear about them right away. It was the Barabbas affair that first caught up with us; the police found out from someone that I spoke Greek and came to my house with so many questions that I thought it best to leave town, or better the province. I still can't give a good account of the political situation, which seemed to change every morning, but I found the harbor at Caesarea crammed with a throng of people, Jews and Phoenicians and Greeks alike, who all had the same idea as me and were trying to jump onto the departing ships. Leaping over a cubit of foul water onto a coastal boat bound for Egypt, I struck an old woman on the back. I landed face down, splayed on the briny deck, and when I lifted my head I saw her thrashing in the sea, with her garments spread like a dark flower to pull her down. No one paid her any attention. For their part, the Egyptians didn't want me on board and left me burnt and blistered with deck work; also a couple of sailors pinned me down to get what they could from my body. Those are my private troubles.

As for the stories that have started to come out of Jerusalem after all this time, I have no way of understanding them. They seem to be playing a sinister game of names with everyone and everything I used to know. There is another Bethania in the stories, over the Jordan where the prophets ate locusts; there is another Maryam who was a whore, another Eleazar who was not a rich man but a beggar covered in sores. There is another Jesus too, a rabbi with my name—though of course the name means nothing, thousands of people in Judea had that name—who went to the grave of another Eleazar, or perhaps my Eleazar, and did the thing I couldn't do. How, I wonder? By sheer force of argument? Or is it only a misremembering of my story? Maryam knew those Galilean prophets, those madmen over the Jordan; she might have called on one of them. All I know is that decades have passed and those times, which seemed evil then, are nothing compared to what we suffer now. Living in Cyprus, an old man, I hear how the legionnaires have leveled the walls of Jerusalem, destroyed the Temple, carried off the menorah to the triumph in Rome. When they breached the last citadel they found a thousand last defenders who had chosen death over torture. And because my people live by laws—because the revolt began for the sake of those laws—those last thousand had slain each other by compact, each in turn, so that only one had to sin in murdering himself.

I still work when I have to, and not long ago I received a wartime Judean coin in Hebrew script, dated year one of the redemption of Israel. I turned it over in my fingers and wondered how they had imagined that redemption. The end of Rome, I suppose. But if Rome is to fall, I very much fear that whatever comes next will be worse. The legionnaires may be apes but they are predictable apes, they understand roads and sewers, and it takes no imagination to think of a hundred worse masters. I haven't led an honorable life. It was wholly against my conscience that I once tried to sell life for the dead. But even I never tried to sell the end of time. The heavenly spheres have ages still to turn, and punishments for us all.

Eurystheus

Dear Herakles. Son of Zeus, beloved of the gods, blood of my blood. Brave in war, generous in peace. Bearer of gifts: sword of Hermes, bow of Apollo, breastplate of Hephaistos, horses of Poseidon, robe of Athena. Dearest Herakles. I don't hate you.

There is justice, and there is injustice, and within justice various shades of injustice, and (this point the subtlest) within injustice various shades of justice. You won't understand this. One curse engenders another, and as they multiply they form a web. The study of webs, having been my life, has earned me the throne of Mycenae. A man, even a strong man, even a strong and courageous man, if walking blindly is likely to blunder into a web, and then the Furies will pursue him until he dies.

You're an able killer, Herakles. I salute you as a killer. The snakes in the cradle were just practice, of course, just infantine high spirits. Now tell me: were you wearing the same happy baby's smile when you cracked open your tutor's skull with a lyre? An instrument of music made a weapon: was that heroic? Was it beloved of the gods? Well, not everyone shares your particular closeness to the gods, not everyone can judge. All the same we must wonder, being experienced, what sort of man throws his wife and three children into the fire. Of course if we do such a thing we are not master of ourselves, we are driven from without, we are mad: that is to say, we haven't made the proper study of webs, we are named after Hera but can't avert her wrath. Now blood balances blood. That is what you're learning. We live in a savage world, Herakles, where closeness to the gods entails closeness to monsters, and often a great distance from the human. The age is past when we could all live off fallen acorns. The arts of planting, the arts of husbandry are not what we could wish—I am speaking now as an administrator. I, and civilization through me, have use for you. You come of your own will to serve me, understanding that you and I are but devices of the gods. I laid no penance on you; you laid it on yourself. You must kill for me.

Consider the lion of Nemea—and don't be misled by words, this is no mountain cat, it is Typhon-spawn, fallen from the moon, suckled by the lady of the moon—as a hideous chthonic force whose ravages have frightened away investors and stunted what could have been the crowning wine region of Hellas. Admirable red grapes in Nemea, so dark, so velvet—but what do you care about viniculture? Problems are so simple in your world! I point out the lion and off you go in pursuit, rip an olive tree from the ground and club the thing senseless and choke out the breath from its invulnerable hide and bring the hide home, dearest Herakles, you shining star, you great virile slab of animate meat. This is what I tell my fellow heads of state: what a boon to have Herakles under me, what a jewel for accomplishing objectives, perhaps not a man to set his own objectives, that's fair, perhaps not equipped for the larger picture, but we each have our endowments and each species of prowess has its slot in the hierarchy, as I have my logical position at the summit of the hierarchy, which is distinct from my physical position in this wine jar. I admit it might not seem a position of command, crouched in a wine jar. It needs some imagination to understand that a king will have abilities different from yours, and different sensitivities as well. So imagine an able and sensitive king, hard at work for the benefit of his city, suddenly interrupted by a subordinate who comes tramping into the hall dressed in the hideous hide of a chthonic demon-lion, practically roaring out his greeting, and you might see how the sensitive king could be obliged to, let's say, redeploy himself into a jar, and it's not yet the optimal time to come out of the jar, and our meetings are going to be delegated from now on. My proxy Kopreas will find you at the city gates, if the Lernaian Hydra doesn't kill you. As for the hide? Dear Herakles, what do I want with the stinking flyblown hide of a moon-monster? Keep the awful thing.

Regretfully, sincerely though delivered by proxy, making heartfelt use of a delegated mouth, I have to bring up an imbalance in your accounts. This can happen in the case of multiple heads. You may examine the documents. Let n denote the number of heads of the Lernaian Hydra, which we will set to an initial value of nine, a good mythic number. Now we posit you, Herakles, approaching with a cloth over your face to block the ninefold poison breath, wielding a sword or sickle or two sickles or whatever you like—we aren't trying to recreate the past, we are only constructing a model—and slicing off a head. Down it goes, sanguinary, into the steaming lake. Reduce n by one. And isn't it satisfying! Who wouldn't love to exercise a strength like yours? But remember, Herakles, your every action is enmeshed in webs. The cosmos turns on laws of requital, each force has its counterforce, and you can't cut through every problem with a bronze blade. From the bloody conic section of the neck sprout two buds, two greenish vines. The monster has a vegetable nature, you thought you were killing an animal but in fact you were fecundating a plant, these two new heads bring n up to ten, so what percentage of the Lernaian Hydra have you actually slain? The unfortunate answer is negative eleven and one-ninth percent. And if you repeat the exercise—slice, gore, bud— again you find n reduced by one, then increased by two, bringing us to eleven, meaning that you have slain another negative ten percent of the Lernaian Hydra, or with respect to the initial value of n, negative twenty-two and two-ninths percent. You may extrapolate the problem from here. A crab is pinching your toe; step on it. You need a counterforce, you need your helper Iolaos to bring the element of fire and torch the cut stems. Good, Herakles. That stanches the growth, it allows you to whittle the forest down to its root, the unkillable seed, the lone immortal head that flops and snaps at you even after you've severed it. Now what do you do with such a problem? Well, you hide it under a rock—that's thinking like an administrator. But this requires a change in the accounting, we have to determine what percentage p of your task is accomplished, because you can't treat limitless things like limited things, to mix them up generates problems, you start to think that one runner can never overtake another, that the flying arrow is at rest—I know you've never been overburdened by thought, Herakles, but follow this. If we incorporate time into our measurements, tracking not heads but head-hours, that is, the amount of time actually lived per hour per head, then the percentage p of head-hours lived by the mortal heads as against the immortal head shrinks to zero. That last head is still dreaming under its rock, ready to flop and snap, to generate another monstrous forest, on the day that rock is moved. Zero percent accomplished, Herakles. And correcting for the help of Ioalos, your personal balance in fact comes to half of zero, a figure so infinitesimal that the Lernaian Hydra has to be considered a wash, it can't count toward your ten tasks, you'll need another.

It's not a joke, Herakles, to say I don't hate you. It's more than words. You're family, and while kingship may complicate a family relation it shouldn't be an obstacle to candor. I know that in a sense I kept you off the throne of Mycenae. And if there were a dozen Mycenaes with a dozen thrones, one for every last male child of our house, then the cosmos would be very different and no one happier than I. What do I want with these labors? What do I gain as a king, as a man, by adding one more animal to my menagerie? Didn't you look into the night sky while you were chasing the hind of Artemis? Didn't you see your adversaries set in the stars—the lion, the hydra? Even the crab? It's Hera who sets them against you, your agon is with her, I'm a mere instrument and I could be your best friend in this affair if you would trust me. But you have a different idea. After a year's pursuit the hind collapses, you take its golden antlers to lead it home, but straight away you have to explain yourself to Artemis. So you hatch a compromise. You call me out to the gates and in my sight you set the hind loose; off it bounds into unknown realms, back to its mistress, so Eurystheus was too slow, no hero he, and no harm done. Only a lesson for the ages in bad faith. The letter of our contract is preserved and its spirit lies in tatters. If you'd trusted me, Herakles, if you'd only spoken to me in advance, we could have found another way. I'm disappointed in you. Not angry. Just disappointed.

A bear? A boar? Out with it! I said out, I'm not coming out of the jar until you take it out, why by the twelve high gods would you drag that thing into my hall? Are you trying to make a point about these animal labors? Because if they're too symbolic for you, too removed from life, there's no shortage of real work around here. Let me see. Let me see. In Elis, across the Peloponnese, my colleague Augeas keeps some stables packed to the rafters with horseshit. Will that do, Herakles? Would you like to go and move a mountain of shit?

You don't understand the nature of work. I realize this now. Listen: if an ordinary worker, a level-headed man of the country, is told to go and move a pile of horseshit, what will he do? He'll pick up his shovel and stick it in the pile. He doesn't fear it. It isn't unclean to him. He takes it as a substance with so much volume and so much weight. He might dry it in the sun, he might burn it for fuel or enrich his fields or line his walls to keep the insects out. To behave otherwise, to shrink from the stuff, is to mark it as forbidden—that is to say, you create a cult, you venerate it, and that's unnatural. Of course in this case the worker won't be taking the horseshit home; it doesn't belong to him, it comes from the king's horses, and the worker is hired only for his prowess with the shovel. It won't be pleasant. It won't be heroic or elevating. That is not the nature of work. The lower strata of the pile will have turned into something like earth, black and bitter, but first to be shoveled is the upper slime fresh from the herd, so reeking hot that you can't breathe around it. The worker stops his throat, shovels all he can, runs out to gulp air from the sky, returns with bursting lungs and shovels again until his vision goes black, then crawls back to open air with ten thousand flies swarming at his face. Is that a low occupation to you? Is it base? You're accustomed to heroics, Herakles, to simple quests with simple goals. Most of us don't have such lives. A thousand things might happen in the course of the stable work. The worker could be told that his working methods displease the lady of the house and that he will have to start carrying the horseshit in unobtrusive handfuls. He could be told that the new location is worse than the old, that he must begin moving his loads from point alpha and point beta to newly designated point gamma. Or he could encounter a second worker who is industriously collecting the ordure just dropped at point beta and carrying it back to point alpha. Or he could be told to quit entirely and go milk goats with his filthy hands. There is no quest, no prize. The worker's only choice is to honor the work itself, to make a god of it, to pick up his portion of dung and carry it like a torch in the mysteries. But you, Herakles, don't even look at the stable before you decide that it degrades you. It's beneath you to touch a shovel, to approach a solitary horse. Instead you walk miles distant and perform another demigod feat and divert a river. Admirable. So long as you don't drown the herd. All you lost was the meaning of the task. You were meant to work, Herakles, you were meant to carry around the horseshit until it became radiant. This wasn't about cleaning the stable floor by sunset—it was about you with a shovel in your hand, grunting and sweating and stinking like a man. And you want to share the reward! You contract with Augeas for a tenth part of his herd, as if you were his equal and not a hired hand. I repeat, you don't understand the nature of work. You may be a demigod, but your human half was born blind and dumb. This labor is rejected. Take your bow, Herakles, take your lion skin and your club and your armful of divine gifts and go back out to hunt sacred animals. What else are you good for?

I was informed. Stymphalian birds, Cretan bull, mares of Diomedes, cattle of Geryon, and all done with strength and cunning I'm sure, but I'm occupied right now, it's not as if I just sit here enjoying grapes and orgasms while you're away, I have a city to run. Shut the door when you go.

Herakles, forgive me. Speak to me. Forget the crown a moment, forget the throne, and let me tell you a private thing. I too dreamed of the Amazons, once. Every boy dreams of them in the twilight of youth, before manhood dawns. In that twilight the city is faint, the walls are made of shadow, the people are shades. They won't stand up to the sun; light erases them. There is no solid thing but the dry land under the city. Only the land returns the sunlight, and only the land is fit to return the boy's love. Of course there may be a man in the city who loves the boy and takes him to bed. And there may be girls in the city whom the boy himself has begun to love. But they are shades against the brilliant land, as the boy's own father and mother are shades, as anything must be a shade which belongs to men and the city built by men, to the laws and customs which the boy does not understand and which seem established only to separate the white-hot land from his white-hot heart. The land is a woman. Or it partakes of woman without partaking of mortality, it is a goddess not like the city's goddess. So the boy goes where no cities are. In a cove of dark water he lashes timbers into a raft and raises the sail. Rocks pierce the shoreline, seaweed-draped and mussel-crusted, as if dropped from heaven, and grass and flowers cover the slopes. High in the wind gulls and crows contend. When the raft is launched the god of wind, who loves the boy, steers him past the clashing rocks and through the Euxine straits. The boy baits a line with dark bread and grows strong and lean on the fish of open water. He will be able to wrestle, to throw the spear and draw the bow, when he arrives at the country of the Amazons. And when he steps from the raft onto the foamed shore, when he finds the Amazons waiting on horseback, arrayed with bows at their sides and their bronze crescent shields glittering in the sun, he sees that their eyes are strong and full of the land as his own eyes are strong and full of the sea; and this moment of encounter, of recognition and balance, of discovering the Amazons to be wild and beautiful mirrors of all that is wild and beautiful in himself, is the utmost point of the dream.

The far side of that encounter no one could imagine. None before you, Herakles. You made that journey not in the twilight of youth but in the full sun of manhood; you stepped onto that shore in solid flesh, in bone and sinew. How is it possible? They call me your rival, but who would rival you for the love of the Amazon queen? If Hippolyte vaults from her steed, light as a falling leaf, and walks barefoot on the sand—if she holds out her sun-darkened arm and leads you to her tent and gives you her golden girdle, then what shall we do but wonder? Wonder and mourn. Our lives are not single or whole, they are plaited with the threads of other lives, and your darkest thread is that curse of Hera which your every breath weaves forward, even inside Hippolyte's tent lit in gold, even where your skin and her skin swim in gold beside the weapons of war. Hera's voice runs through the camp, crying treachery; the Amazons draw their bows. And when you sink your sword into Hippolyte's side—when her blood spills, dark gold, over the golden sand—you must hear some echo of your wife and children screaming in the fire. It can't be unwritten. I weep for it too, in my way. But you should see how my daughter loves the girdle. She holds it to her waist, turns in front of the bronze mirror, picks up a reed and stretches it like a bow and laughs. My eyes cloud when I watch her. I'll leave you now.

Eight years and a month we've been at this, Herakles; one great year, as the physicists count it, for your time of expiation. I feel much older. I have a hard time remembering how it was at the beginning. I must have envied you, I must have feared you as well, but it all seems so distant. I'm tired. I've been running behind since my birth, ever since Hera pushed me into the world before my time to keep any son of Zeus from ruling Mycenae. I told you once before that we were tools of the gods, but I didn't know then what it meant. Only now, at the middle of life, have I learned to feel the cold hand of the divine around my body, gripping me morning and night, hollowing me out from the inside. I've seen it around you as well, pulling you back from your labors wearier each time. And no doubt you've had the worst of it. But I begin to disbelieve in you and me as separate creatures. The longer we persist as tools in the hands of others, the more we hollow out to empty names, and in the webs of the gods, the starry designs of ages, it is very hard to say where one name stops and another begins. I'm so tired, Herakles. I can't imagine what you think of me. Why don't you speak? Those calculations which I thought were mine, discounting two of your labors and setting you two more, I now think must have come from outside. Why the number twelve compels us, why it has installed itself as occult law, I don't know. But here are the last two. Golden apples from the world's end, and Kerberos brought up from hell. Go and finish this.

I can't touch it, Herakles. I can't even look at it. It curves like heaven. Every point flawless, identical to every other point; the eye approaches, strikes the surface and slides away. Even you and I are identical so long as we regard the apple, the apple equates us, we are the apple regarding itself. Do you understand why it was the shapeshifter Nereus who revealed the garden to you? Why you had to wrestle him through each of his shapes? One thing in all. And don't you long for it? Sweet unity—how the thought swells my tongue. I know, even to set them on earth is forbidden, what sacrilege, ages of torment, worse than Prometheus on his rock. But my tongue. Oh, take them away, let Athena take them, we've had too much traffic with the gods. Why don't you speak to me, Herakles? Are you really going silent into hell?

Up at dawn, then, for the sacrifice. The sun a burning face over the mountains as always, its light doubled in the sea. And you too ignore me, sun? I'm not one of your children? The priests behind me chanting for Hera, the white bull with garlanded horns. We led it between the columns to the open altar, where it snorted and rolled its eyes. I hate their movements; their breath too frightens me. When they cut its throat it knelt, dropping its head, then the front legs, then the rear. Torches were brought. When the blood began to smoke I said, "That's the end for you, bull-god of Crete. No more of your sort in the new age. No more crudities, no more monsters in the temples." And I who had been given charge of monsters, what place was mine? I left the priests to stir the flames and walked back to the great hall with attendants at my heels. They'll never leave me, not while I wear the crown, but they keep silent as the gods. That deep sky of morning, marine wind in the cypress, the diving swallows: all part of my kingdom, none of it mine. In the late morning there was an execution to witness. Distant claimants to the throne still appear from time to time, branches of our house so obscure that no verse will sing their names. The young man knelt proudly, kept his proud head high, fell forward after the knife was pulled from his breast. The blood of Perseus. Cicadas in the courtyard, the white city below and flocks of sheep on the far hills. I took a bowl of spiced wine and went back to the bedchamber, where you waited, beloved wife, at your mirror. Do you remember how we came together? Do you remember how long we slept? But I woke alone. Something was missing in me, as if I'd forgotten my name. Your blanket was warm but you were nowhere. The air had turned damp and dark, the wind keened outside, gray clouds scudded through the sky. An attendant waited at the door to arrange my robes and beard before I went out to the throne. "Why the dark?" I asked. "A storm off the sea?" He looked away, embarrassed—they were always embarrassed at not speaking—and moved his hands over my clothes. No daylight touched the hall. Torches were lit at the door and the old relief sculptures danced on the walls, horses' necks and chariot wheels and grandfather Perseus going after the monsters, looking out hour by hour to ask what sort of Perseus was I. In the firelight the hall seemed deeper than ever, the throne too large for me, built for other limbs. "Where is my wife?" I asked. "My daughter?" The attendants exchanged a worried look, as if each expected the other to answer. "Then find the priests of Hera," I said, "have them explain," and they departed and the hall lost its balance. Earthquake, I thought; the gods are shaking the earth. And I would have understood even this, if only that thing were not missing from my head. When the shaking ceased I found a torch at my hand. Outside the white city had turned gray, spilling down the mountain like a wave breaking against the walls. The clouds rolled overhead like a second sea. A cold wind struck me, I lifted my hands and found the torch extinguished. I tossed it away and started down the slope with my arms extended, the whole city now off balance, all the walls pointing the wrong way. The attendants were nowhere, the priests were nowhere, no one was on the streets at all. Where were my people? I stopped at a house, put my face to the window and saw no hearth, no bed, the floor not swept. Dry grass sprouted in the corner and roots crawled up the walls. I stumbled on with the wind playing games around me, stirring the dirt and leaves against each other. Everything was in worse repair than I remembered; nothing looked lived in. Had I not been attending to this? Thinking of the monsters, of the gods, had I neglected to administer part of my city? The priests would know. It was one thing to be thought a tyrant, but if they thought me a fool in the bargain, an incompetent governor—these roads were unwalkable. Grass everywhere, hillocks tripping the feet. I wasn't even sure that this was the main avenue; it might have been a side path running between the fallen walls. In places they had vanished to the foundations, exposing the base stones and drainage channels that were never meant to be seen. I took up a piece of timber for a staff—had it been part of a wall, of a roof? The clouds had sapped the daylight, and when I looked behind me I saw only a gray sheet, as if rain had come up. Where were the city gates? Roofs open everywhere to the sky, the walls mere sketches of worn stone, thick with blossoming weeds. They had hidden this district from me; they had let it fall apart under my rule, just to tarnish my name. On the path before me lay a bone. It was small and elongated, very pale in the faint light; it might have come from a fox or cat, perhaps a human hand. I knelt to take it, heard snarls and lifted my eyes to Kerberos. Six black eyes rolled at me, three snouts huffed the air and yapped, uncountable teeth flashed from the black lips. It wasn't one animal but a pack of animals, not one thing but a deadly confusion of things—it was the apple's inverse, the sign of collapse, and only the iron arms of Herakles clasped around its middle could hold it together. The lower world had been wrenched from its place, and now it strained against Herakles's grasp—the snake tail, the nest of heads—breathing air it wasn't made for, scratching alien earth. "Herakles!" I cried. He didn't answer. I stepped forward, abject, placing my hope in his grip, and I saw his face. I wish I hadn't. His eyes were lost in the storm, his jaw set, every muscle strained with the labor of upending the world. He had knocked the cosmos on its back, he held Death prisoner in his arms, and now he was receiving his reward for this last labor, that second death which the gods give to very few. He was turning into his name. The hero's end is to be pulled out of time and into that place where every city is a ruin, every man a tomb, every deed another song for the generations to learn and forget and alter beyond recognition. The hero looks down from the stars where his shape has been set, immutable, and condemned to change with each eye that beholds him. Paralyzed, all sculpture, Herakles wrestled the hell-dog at the heart of our wrecked city. It would never break free. He would never let it go. Enough! Enough! I dropped to my knees. And when my eyes opened—sweet mercy. I was back in our bedchamber, back in the warm blood of time. Your head lay on my shoulder. Antimakhe. How light your breath. How soft your uncoiffed hair. Sleep on. He'll trouble us no more. The songs are his, the stars are his, but those are a spume playing over the real things of earth, they mean nothing. We'll have no more torment from the gods. We'll eat and drink, we'll see our daughter grow. Oh love, I thought this was never to end, I thought these curses would follow us to our tombs, but the tale is over. We have a home.

PHILOMELA

To understand the speech of birds:

Sing fair, sing by kind, outside of mind. Three families, three tribes. Hoopoe, crest of war. Swallow, remorse in the rafters. Nightingale, the tongue that sings.

Sing, tongue. Once where hurt we were hurt.

This is not remembering. Following paths of insects. Under the beehive, the wasp's nest, dead grubs rest grounded: quick, into the beak. Food to carry nestward, children to feed, they grow, not all. Strong children we fledge and sing to strong children. By sun and moon, but hard to hear by sun. Too much heard by sun.

Close the eye of day. Thin clouds roll the moon up the sky. Under leaves we shelter from raindrops, clutch twigs, sing. The speech of birds is not speech. A child gurgles birdspeech before it grows a mind. Grown into mind it feels the mind's exile, is exiled all its life until at last the gods fray the mind. And under the pain of fraying is the sweet return to birdspeech, to moon and sun and seasons. Sing, tongue.

In childhood, half bird, we stood in a stone room. Beside our father and sister we saw him enter: bronze beard, bronze helm, horsehair crest. A lone step brought him to our sister. His hand caught hers.

He is king of Thrace. He reigns.

We hadn't understood. But when his hand caught hers, when she brought down her proud head, eyes closed, to rest herself on his power, we did understand: that was to reign. So we found our tongue and stepped from the world into the mind's exile, bird no more.

Gone many years he returned, then, for us. He walked long with father in the colonnade, spoke low, deliberation always between them like an iron bar, him always pushing and father frowning in his beard, weeping out his white beard, too weak to hold it back. When the bar fell nothing stood between him and us. He took a lone step. In the colonnade, beautiful, we knew we were beautiful, linen at our hips, gold linked around our neck and plenitude of words on our tongue. Father took our hand and joined it to his. Our head dropped. His reign began.

With the hoopoe we have no commerce. No commerce with the swallow. Nothing in their swoop, their feathered flash, their mud and dung nests. Outside of mind is no commerce. Birdspeech alone.

But where is our sister? Debarked on rock and bracken, the sea spraying our heels, we asked: where is our sister? He smiled. Did he fear? It seemed he feared, but one cannot reign and fear, so his smile had another name. He hungered. Wind tossed his helm's crest, swayed the tips of pines. Wild grass sprang pathless between the rocks. In the sky nothing flew. He said:

Come into the house.

What happened in the lonely house. Sing, tongue. Our blooded scrap of mind. Writhed naked and living on the earth. So long.

Stripped of linen, of gold, of words. So long.

Once where hurt we were hurt.

Where shadowed twig and leaf streak sunlight we heap dry grass. Lay a ring of dry oak leaves, velvet moss within, stiff grass, soft down. Four eggs, five eggs, leaf green. Till they crack, sing to keep them whole. Till they crack, sing to drive other songs away. Let no strange singer spy the leaf-green eggs.

Then was the end of words. No end of life. We had air, we had water and coarse bread from our woman keeper, we could not step from the lonely house. He never returned. Night spilled over day and day spilled out of night and he did not return. At noon we lay naked on the floor and gazed at slants of light, took water in our mouth and spat it out. The mind tried to fray then. It tested its own weave, pulled its own warp threads in search of fray. But no. One morning we surfaced from fever and saw dawn's rose above the walls, heard shadows of words in our mind. Our keeper came with water. We made signs:

Bring a loom.

Loom and thread. I'll weave for you. To do anything with these hands.

She brought a measure of thread. A Thracian loom. We made small things first, hand-cloths and neck-cloths, to coax more wool. Then came a measure of white, a measure of purple, matter enough for something beautiful. It would not bear doing, to remake him and ourself, unless it were beautiful. So we cast onto the loom the word-shadows in our mind:

Tereus, I remake you. Not because you deserve this doubled life, not because these things should be rewoven in purple, but because your hand has pressed its shape into my mind and so long as I move in the mind I will move in your hand's shape. I remake it. We wove in half light for secret weeks, fevered at the lit wick, till all was done and we took the weave from the loom and bundled it, figures hidden, to give with signs to our keeper. For the palace. The queen of Thrace.

A dozen of dozens of songs. Cheechew, sharp and quick, chirchir chirchir, the long whistle wewew wuit. Throat's rattle, jug jug jug, beak's buzz, high flowing tereu tereu. Each song is the only song while sung. Each second another song rises. Jug jug grig grig. Cheechit peleu. Tereu. Sing, tongue.

Disguised, crowned in ivy, our sister came with revelers in hides. For her the door was opened, but when she stepped into the lonely house we were shamed, we tried to run. She caught us, covered us in ivy and ivy's smell, took us away. Why don't you speak, she asked.

Shame pressed our eyes. We let drop our mouth. She saw.

On the long homeward path, all along the rock and bracken, she spoke:

Hurt him.

How can we hurt him.

Fire the palace.

Cut his throat.

Sever his parts. Make him eat—

Wind, owl's scream. Disguised, under torches, we came by night to the palace. In the colonnade their son laughed and turned somersaults, five years old, pink flesh on his limbs' long bones.

Oh there, said sister. If he hungers.

Speechless we nodded. Once where hurt raped with sword in the mouth. Once hurt ever hurt.

A wasp draws a heavy line in the air. Moths flap errandless over dark leaves. Beetles graze the earth, testing ridges of soil with spindled legs, then blur their wingcases and are gone. Hop, head cocked: snap the beak. The hard parts crunch against the tongue, snap again till the hardness shatters over flesh, cock the head, swallow. Slow moths are quick to take, circling gnats quick to take, a dozen or more hardly felt in the throat. The grasshopper and stag beetle will fight for release. Not so the worms and grubs, the soft blind meat. Swallow one and carry the second home, rich prize.

Hidden, a snake in shadow, we waited in the feast hall. Wool wrapped a stone in our hands. All servants withdrawn, sister alone led her husband to his banquet chair. The feast of Bacchus. Master's food, the wife to serve. In the firelight we watched him sit, waiting for his dish, heavy and old and at peace. He was strange to us. The hungry smile whose shape had pressed our mind was gone. Had it extinguished his hunger to hurt us? Was it a thing he needed to do only once? This old man in linens, this thick face cloaked in ash-bronze beard, had forgotten hunger's shadow.

Sister brought the hot dish. He chewed. How we'd spiced it! As girls in Athens we'd seen the Arabian ships bringing cassia and cinnamon, we'd learned the arts of burnt powders. Let him chew. Without haste he raised the joint to his teeth and tore flesh lightly from bone. His was leisure to taste. Our sister knelt beside him, watched him swallow, offered the cloth for his lips and tempted him to stretch his comfortable belly, to loosen his limbs in the chair, till he spoke as he must:

Where is my son? Call my son in.

Laughter jarred in her throat. So long she'd waited to speak that her own voice now frightened her. Was it her alone, was it the voice inside her that bid her stand and lift her head and extend her arm to the dish—

Whom you seek is within you!

What could that old face do in its comfortable beard? It blinked in hurt, turned pale green eyes down to its belly, wondering, feeling the flesh of its flesh melt back to the old seed. She laughed and there was nothing in the laugh, it had outrun its message, and we in the corner waited for his face to twist into a first question, a first understanding that he would pass the rest of his life in a dark tunnel. Then we leapt forward and flung the wool weave to cast the child's head, blood-crust and staring eyes, into his lap.

Flight. Down the palace steps and into the wild he chased our bloody robe and heels. The table lay toppled in the hall. In his hand flashed a blade. The cosmos streaked blood, his guts spun in him while his tongue moved unhooked from his will, still licking round the mouth and liking what it tasted. It had no words. There was no word for this flight while bearing a dark tunnel around him, his cry for revenge with no revenge to match, desperation, briars, the Furies. His mouth gaped empty, wanting the word, pulling from his face in search of the absent word; then it was lost, melted into wild. That was the fraying of mind. What remained was the path his mouth had taken, a slope of beak; he tossed his crest, spread his feathers and was gone. We were gone, frayed into flight. Blue light before dawn. Empty glade.

In nature nothing melancholy. Nor were we born for death. But joy too is cold. There is no remembering; we fall from shadow to shadow and cannot tell what shadows they were. One song erases another, one flash of wing gathers to itself all of time. We take worms in the beak and worms take our unfledged children. The species will change its shape. Follow clouds and rain, shadow to shadow, blank glow of sun each day renewed. Such is the end of weeping. Such is the speech of birds.

Ragnarök

Hughes will betray us, though we don't know how. We don't know anything. His hair is red: is that why? It bristles like copper, the same color as his freckles, when he opens his mouth you expect to see copper teeth in there, his blood must run copper, it must marble his bones. His eyes as well. They change color. Some call them red, some green, this can start arguments. It can't be denied, the office has been tense since the auditors came in. But we need Hughes. And that's the difficult thing, that we can't trust anyone else with his job, that it has to be him who gets the applications off the server. Because we have to keep the applications in the server, they have to ripen there, on account of how the applicants bring them in. It's a scandal. The standard form is on the books for anyone to look up: it must be cubical, it must be partitioned, it must employ three orthogonal axes of rotation and five colors of the spectrum plus white. Those are the requirements, and nothing ever comes within a mile of them. The usual thing is a stone, sometimes rough-hewn into geometric form, sometimes not, etched with marks that, we suppose, carry a kind of personal significance for the applicant, though they never mean anything to us. The boy at the front desk will have to explain that this object doesn't count, procedurally, as an application of any kind; the applicant will growl and wave; and so it goes until the senior clerk, who doesn't care what the intake looks like, pushes his cart in from the back room, permits the object to be dumped into the bin and wheels it down to the basement, where by slow degrees it will be digested into structured data and come out as a workable cube. The mystery of the server. Opening the basement door you meet darkness: then warm air, oily damp on your skin and a sweet-sour ferment at the back of your throat. Your ears catch an ocean of distant clicks. Throw the switch. A bulb fires above you, casting your shadow forward on the rock floor and lighting, though only in outline, the opening of the pit. Here the ash tree sends down its roots from the courtyard, and the server has built itself around them: a deep network of passages, no one knows how deep, carved by the drones that move in a fever at the pit's edge. They swarm past and over each other, half in shadow, bumping translucent bodies, raking their limbs and quivering feelers in each other's faces, ruminating data packets in their jaws. At bottom, we understand, is where the queen twists against her earth casing, answering queries from the client computers upstairs, devouring old drones and birthing the new. Of course no one can claim to have seen her—except the Old Man, who claims a lot of questionable things—and our evidence for the queen's existence is simply that the office is still running, that something has been managing our records all this time. Even Hughes's description of the basement we have to take on faith. He'll explain his technique if you ask him, though he can't do it without mockery. You move forward, he says. You tilt your head, squint against the dimness, and you'll see drones break from the murk. They clatter up to you and stop, quivering their feelers at the light; that's when you join your fists and knock one on the head. The body will shake, the head will bob a little, the feelers might whip your arms, if your skin starts to crawl just take a breath and keep knocking till the mandibles drop the cube. Pick it up, quick—you'll find it hot and slimed over—and get back to the door before the drone starts moving. That, says Hughes, is how you get the data; and no one quite believes him, but no one's worked up the courage to go and look for themselves. Even the stoutest skeptics will admit the data isn't a pretty thing on its own terms. You don't want to face it naked. Better to stay upstairs with the bright folders and icons on your screen, the cartoons that pop up to help you search for files. Yes, we'd be sunk without Hughes. But he'll betray us. How do we know? The same way he knows, the same way everyone knows, some kinds of knowledge you don't air in public, you'd be an idiot to open your mouth. The end of the office is already sketched out, at least in broad strokes. Most of us know by name who will kill us. It doesn't help. Usually you can't put a face to the name, and you don't know what to expect beforehand; anyway there's no telling how long until it happens. The distance between now and then seems always to be growing, like a math trick, the office can be in perpetual decline without ever reaching the point of collapse. It must be hardest on people like Hughes, who will actually get a lot of power when the collapse comes. He'll steer the ship of nails, he'll father the wolf that eats the sun. But for now he has to sit at his desk and work on application cubes like everyone else. A few twists will bring five green squares to the same side, but that will stack the reds against each other, and to line them up would scatter the yellows. It's never a quick process. You have to follow a system, you have to enter an intuitive zone, easier on some days than others. It could make anyone dream of devouring the sun. Still it doesn't affect us so badly, somehow we stay loyal to the office even in its current condition. It must be admitted that the empire stopped expanding a long time ago, and nowadays it doesn't seem even to be holding its frontiers. An awful sort of low-grade paper has started to appear in the copier, thin and gray like newsprint and smearing anything you print on it. The soda cans in the fridge tend more and more to bottom-shelf brands. We used to have bottles of sparkling water in there, then they were replaced by a cooler stand that quivered and belched whenever anyone touched it, now there's only a photocopied sign asking us to make do with tap water. We can use as many ice cubes as we like, says the sign, if we remember to refill the freezer tray. Sometimes these measures are announced at staff meetings. No one will show any reaction except the office assistant. Either out of rectitude or out of ignorance, she asks a lot of questions that no one else will: for instance, why so many applications have gone missing. No one wants to think about the missing applications. The Old Man wants to talk about excellence, about how the office can become more excellent. He has an initiative, apparently his own idea, to educate the public about the application requirements, so that they'll start using the proper format and relieve the front desk from its endless intake of stones. Management has jumped all over the idea. If the public can be taught to format cubes, says someone, couldn't they be taught to solve them as well; but that idea gets quickly deflected, since if the public starts solving its own cubes it's not clear what would keep the office busy. No, the thing is to communicate the standards. The Old Man's single open eye darts around the room, his lips quiver in his beard, words come quick and breathy out of his barrel chest. We have suggestions too, there could be posters, radio spots, a website; we want to help outfit the dream, but the Old Man isn't listening to us, the dream is his and he resents anyone encroaching on it. It's only when he runs out of breath that the floor opens to questions, and that's when the assistant raises her hand and says okay, but what about the missing applications. Everyone makes pained faces. No one wants to say the obvious thing, that applications go missing when they can't be solved. Finally one of the managers suggests that it might not be a high priority item for today, and the assistant says all right, but there's a field for the missing applications on her spreadsheet, something has to be marked on the spreadsheet, and the manager says he understands that, but it's not a high priority today, more of a moderate to low priority, and the assistant says, fine, do you just want me to stop reminding you, and the manager looks worried and says no, not at all, it's excellent that you're reminding us, only perhaps we should take it off the priority calendar. Okay, says the assistant, so when do you want me to bring it up again. Maybe, says the manager without conviction, maybe in a month. Fine, says the assistant, in a month, and sits back and crosses her arms. Sometimes we feel uneasy that it's our only woman who gets these jobs, that it's she who has to answer the phone and stock the fridge with soda. What if it's unjust, what if we have to answer to somebody. But this worry can't hold our attention for long, like all of our worries it grabs us and then it drops away. It's true that we're attracted to the assistant. It isn't a sexual feeling, there's no sex in the office, but our senses get amplified. Outside we wouldn't notice her. She wouldn't look like anything on television. But in these meetings we stare at her forearms. They're smooth, dark. Does she put lotion on them? Does she wear a scent? Or is it the natural spice of her hair? Does she know we watch her ass when it goes down the hall? When you greet her she's shy, she doesn't smile, but in meetings she's fierce, expecting answers to her awkward questions, when she lifts a finger to her mouth she looks truly intelligent, as much as anyone can look intelligent in here. The light is unkind. It shows up weird hairs on our temples, it blotches our cheeks and wrinkles our eyes into squints. Management looks worst of all, like a bunch of paunchy gray vultures, it makes you wonder how they ever got to run an empire. Was it dishonest? They must have committed some crime, probably long ago. You can't imagine them doing it now. And Hughes must have helped them. He gets to sit up front in the meetings, he smirks and his eyes shine: copper green, copper red. Well, I love the proposal, he says, what an idea, imagine the public bringing in nice clean fabricated cubes, now all you need is a grant to get them some lathes and injection molds. Does management know he's laughing at them? Should we say something? We don't want to cause an upset, everything's been tense since the auditors came in. They're children. Well, they must have degrees and so on, but they look about twelve. Rosy, suntanned, smooth. Monstrously tall. They come bouncing up to you like a pack of happy dogs, it's terrifying. You can't tell the boys apart from the girls, they all have the same strong shoulders, they all giggle. It drives you mad, wondering what they're giggling about over in the spare office while they go through our finances. Surely it's not about us. Surely everything's a joke to them. They've plugged in a stereo and play Bob Marley all day, it carries through the HVAC, suddenly everyone's office has tiny drums and guitars coming out the ceiling vents. No one says anything. Management is truly terrified of them, you can see it in their eyes. We've started ordering out for lunch with company funds—pizza, noodles, wings—and when the food arrives the Old Man will personally take it in to the auditors. "Pizza!" he bellows, in his jolliest voice, and everyone has a laugh. But how much can they find out? What kind of records does the server keep? We don't know. You can't even tell who's been doing the work. When a cube is solved—and never mind what you hear, they really are solved sometimes—it loses its necessity. Its purpose was to be solved, once it's solved that purpose is abrogated, the surprising thing would be if it could persist in its form. It decoheres. The colors were simply guides to the geometry, and they vanish once the geometry is settled; likewise the geometry was simply a method of structuring the color, and without the color it too disappears. You're left with a stone, the same stone that was first brought in, only without the markings. We toss it out front, into the landscaping. There's no point in keeping them around. They don't prove anything, anyone could go out front and pick up an armful if they wanted. It takes a while for this lesson to sink in: that even with all the side effects of our work, there is absolutely no way to track productivity. This despite the fact that working on a cube will demonstrably slow down time; or to phrase it more carefully, without metaphysics, it slows the clocks in the room. It's a curious effect, many theories about how it happens, and of course it interests management since it ought to serve as a benchmark. But since the clocks are circular and the numbers only go up to twelve, in practice two workdays of supreme effort which move the clock only four hours can't be distinguished from two wholly idle days that move it by sixteen. So it all amounts to this: some of us might have solved hundreds of cubes, some not a one, and you can't tell who is who. Naturally it's frowned on to ask. Which doesn't mean we don't try to find out. Even with the best intentions—and one does start with good intentions—you can't do honest work all day. From the outside it's surprising that it should be so tedious, you'd think that working the cubes would be a cushy affair, you get to apply problem-solving skills, make use of your intuition, it's not as dull as data entry, not as cutthroat as sales, certainly not like digging ditches all day. There's a professional culture, we have conferences, debate different approaches: some are convinced that you should organize colors in pairs, others insist it's best to go row by row. There's merit in each position. And yet. After days and weeks of rotating the colored squares they start to lodge in your head; close your eyes at night and they're waiting inside your lids; when you wake in the dark, half dreaming, needing to use the bathroom, it will seem that your bathroom trip must correspond to one of the six colors. Some days you never wake properly at all, your mind is waterlogged, you stare at your cube from inside an aquarium or as if watching a movie from the worst seat in the house, far to one side of the screen so that everything is tilted and foreshortened. Your hands end up working, or appearing to work, all on their own, while your mind slips its tether and floats off to careen from the white walls and ceiling, shuddering with the faint pulse of the light and catching the periodic click, like a clock chime, of your neighbor opening another can of diet soda—how can anyone drink so much diet soda?—and the shuffle of his feet as he walks yet again to the bathroom, once an hour or more, running gallons of caffeinated water through his kidneys just for the fun of it, because after a few weeks even getting up to use the bathroom becomes a reprieve and a reward. How does Hughes cope? There are rumors that under his smirk he's terribly depressed. People say they've overheard him actually talking to himself at his desk, whispering: I've given this office my best years… it will take the rest before I've lived them out… can't separate myself from the office even in thought… it's lodged in my body… grown to fill my core… nothing moves outside it but wisps of limbs… he'll whisper this, people say, and then he'll start to cry. It's a little hard to believe. Maybe they've invented a script and given him their own speaking part. When you glance at his desk he seems to be working, at least his hands are turning a cube, but he has side projects as well. We don't know if management authorizes them. There haven't been consequences. He's been weaving a net. The thread is pale, very fine, seemingly very strong, synthetic-looking, something like fishing line. The pattern is tacked up half finished on his office wall, gossamer-thin at some points and then bunching into knots, hypnotically wrapping itself. You can't predict the structure at any given point, but somehow it seems very familiar. Some of us think it's related to the cubes, that the thread is braided to mimic the series of twists needed to solve a cube and that the entire net is a master map of every possible solution; so if Hughes completes the net, and if he explains the code to management, then the office would start running itself and we'd all be out of a job. That might be paranoid. Anyhow he hasn't shown it to anyone but the office assistant. A couple of times we've seen her in his office, bent forward with a dark finger on her chin, intelligently frowning at the weave; and Hughes leaning over her shoulder, telling her who knows what with that coppery glint in his eye. Is this the kind of thing the auditors want to know about? They've started calling us in for interviews. One by one we go into the spare office, the door is shut and the rest of us loiter outside, trying to be discreet as we peek sideways through the half-drawn blinds at the seated interviewee, hunched forward with white shirtsleeves on the table, and the auditors pacing around him, leaning on the furniture, tossing around a bean bag and giggling between their questions. We can't hear what the questions are. Once the interviewee is out we swarm him: what did they say, how much do they know. At first he can't answer, he's breathless and pale and has to

sit back down, though not—he explains after a minute—because of
the questions themselves. The questions aren't about anything. It's not
about the finances, not about our jobs, except in the broad sense that
everything, somehow, relates to the finances and our jobs. All right, we
say, so what are the questions; nothing, he says, really nothing, it's just
awful how they ask them. Imagine stepping into a room, he says, with
a pack of hunting dogs, all bulk and teeth, friendly of course, they run
up to you panting and wagging their tails, without the faintest idea
that you aren't just another dog; they don't know that you can't bite and
tug, that they could tear off your arm in an eyeblink, and your only
hope is to grin and romp with them. Your fear is the only thing that
could spoil the fun, among the dogs themselves it's all fellowship and
sport, and the feeling grows more and more dire that you alone, in
your fear, in your weakness, harbor the possibility of disaster, you keep
grinning and romping but every moment it's worse and the urge boils
up to shout, to give yourself away, to confess everything. Confess what,
we ask. That you're not a dog, he says, that you're built too weak for
these games. All right, but that wasn't the real question; what we want
to know, what nobody can tell us, is whether we've done anything really wrong. Personal phone calls on company time, admitted; Internet
browsing, not much of it pornographic or illegal; the inability to spend
all of our time, or even much of our time, working the cubes in good
faith; the suspicion that perhaps, in the end, nothing depends on the
cubes. And if these are real crimes? If we are reprimanded, sanctioned,
actually turned out of the office? What then? Some think we'd have no
choice but to become applicants ourselves: we'd start carving our worries as private symbologies into stones, carrying them to the front desk
and badgering the boys there until the intake cart shows up; then, as

the doors close behind it, we'd be left to hope that one day someone upstairs will pick up our cube and begin to work it out. We don't know what happens to the applicants at that point. Maybe nothing happens at all, maybe the connection is severed as soon as the application is dropped off, or maybe the server degrades it. No one's ever come back to inquire after an application, at least we don't think anyone's shown up twice, though admittedly they all look the same to us. They have beards, or if they're clean-shaven they still have the aspect of bearded people, a superfluity of hair pouring from under their beat-up caps, always dark blue caps with worn bands, they're dressed up and down in faded blue, something like overalls, perhaps it's necessary for the work they do. Their lives must be harder than ours, and yet it must also be more free outside the office, more rewarding; you move at your own behest, what little you have is all your own. But perhaps that's wrong, perhaps outside the office it goes worse. Hughes is skeptical. I've been out there, he says. I've seen how the applicants live. You bunch wouldn't last a week. How do you like the thought of crouching over a radiator? Riding the city bus? Eating freeze-dried potato flakes? Why, he asks, do you think the applicants spend so much time on their applications? Do you think their lives are complete or whole— that their lives are even tolerable? No, after a week you'd come back begging to the office, and naturally the office wouldn't have anything to do with you, you'd have to take a different job at a worse office, one of those places where they pay you an hourly rate instead of a salary, time your bathroom breaks, spy on your computer, firewall the Internet, confiscate your cell phone—Hughes is lying, say some of us, there can't really be offices like that, but most of us darkly suspect that such offices are not only possible but necessary. It's only Hughes who doesn't fear them. He must have something juicy on management, he must be planning to rescue himself. He hasn't gone in for an interview yet, but he's been making friends with the auditors. At lunchtime, after they all collect their pizza, he invites them into the courtyard. We've seen them picnicking there, under the ash tree, and afterward Hughes will stand and knock playfully at its smooth gray bark. Sometimes a squirrel will scold him from the branches, he'll laugh, and we'll overhear him teasing the auditors, saying isn't this a fine tree, a strong and solid tree, and then he leans his ear close as if inviting them to listen. Of course they don't get up. But if they did? Would they hear the sound from below, the distant clicks? What we're starting to suspect, what seems likelier all the time, is that the auditors don't know about the server, and management doesn't want them to find out. The server must be illegitimate somehow, frankly we're terrified of the server, the underground queen might keep the office running but the mere idea of her gives us nightmares. And management will have to answer for it. I'd like to see them all led out in handcuffs, says one of us; don't be an idiot, says someone else, it's not them who will get sacrificed. We all make sour faces and nod. And yet most of us do feel loyal to management, they're like parents, you might disdain them but you can't bear to see them upset, they loom so close in the room, their hot breath fills the air, what if they make a scene and start crying, it would be intolerable. Can we let Hughes betray them? Betray us? It will happen whenever his interview happens, we're sure of it, he'll spill everything as soon as the door is shut. Then is the last day at hand? It doesn't seem right, the last day is about us and our enemies, but not these children auditors, they came out of nowhere, they're upsetting our comprehension of things. And Hughes knows it. In the break room, in the bathroom, he drops terrible hints, asking: suppose there is no last day? That's ridiculous, we say, there has to be a last day. Well, says Hughes, rolling his copper eyes skyward, it's a last day for management, for the empire they built—but suppose the idea of a last day is part of their empire as well? Suppose as they fade out, the last day fades out with them, leaving nothing but a blank row of days and years, all identical, stretching into eternity? You can't deny they're fading. Look how *old* they are, Hughes whispers, they'll never fight another battle, they're turning into air. And you know who's going to inherit the earth, is the auditors. The triumph of youth. If you were smart, you might throw your lot in with *them*—and Hughes chuckles, turns on the hand dryer and departs, leaving us an agony of questions. What if he's right? What if we're not going to kill and be killed? We couldn't take it. The office could collapse, it could burn to the ground, that we wouldn't mind, but if the last day is going to be taken from us, if time is going to be flattened out for good, then we have to take steps. Hughes can't be allowed that interview. His net would make a hell of a snare. He's crafty, he has powers, but there are more of us; the auditors wouldn't know, even management could be kept in the dark. They've used him but they don't love him, they wouldn't go looking. Someone needs to call the freight elevator that leads from the ground floor to the basement, and someone needs to wait there with the door held open while the rest of us spread the net and catch Hughes off guard, in the back hall or the bathroom, with six or seven it shouldn't be hard, we wouldn't even have to knock him out, we could just stuff something in his mouth for as long as it takes to get him into the elevator and down to the server room. Then we'll see what's behind that door. If his stories are lies, we'll have his body as a hostage—but all the better if they're true. Server, structure, hive: the drones might kill him at once, but on the other hand they might keep him alive a long while, the machine might even find some new use for him. It's all the same to us, so long as he stays packed away. The machine uses us all, we know that, there's no solution as simple as twisting a cube, but we didn't invent it, we just have to get by. We don't know anything. Except that we'll muddle through: we're sure of this much, we'll find a way to muddle through.

ROMULUS

I

NASCITVR ROMVLVS in anno of his own making
    self-engendering
        creates his circumstance:

II

"I must be preceded so—
    lore of Aeneas and his line,
lust for what is set apart,
    adumbrations of the divine.
Give me a virgin with suitable pudor.
Give me prophecy and a god in the corner."

III

It is attested that from the hearth of the king issued
    an apparition of arms
        and a virile form,
    which remained some days in the household.
Honor to the king! He proposed coupling between his daughter

and the virile form,
        be it accomplished

FIAT

(unless the daughter refused and they had to bring in a maid)

FIAT

"There shall be no waste of apparitions;
        their lusts and ours must flow in one channel.
Something consummate the virile form—"

EXIT MARS

IV

From something's belly sprung a prodigy.
        Two heads and four legs.
                Infants tell nothing, they are pure seed: but *these*!

As if men of deeds were mirrored in the babes,
        as if mirrors turned on deeds to come
                cast backward in unnatural eyes
        of unnatural thick-thewed infants.

        A vine has sprouted.
                Cut it.

V

ROMVLVS self-engenders:

DICITVR

"The river flowed over into which we were cast.
    Time's torrent held us and did not devour.
Washed up at the fig tree,
      we lay on our backs, and our infant sexes
          pointed nowhere in the breeze.
A lupa, common whore, bowed over us,
      shaded us with her hair,
      dangled her teats in our faces.
Birds left us food."

VI

In this wise (says the scholiast)
      the earth acquires its king.

We mark his coming and the division of time:
      first the eternity of kingless earth, fallow in its sun,
      then the commencement of war and aqueducts.

Remus troubles us. Two-headed birth
      we understand, but the prodigy in later life,
          after the king splits himself and slays himself,
      is vexatious.

The stories branch without confluence and comfort not.
How many eagles over the Palatine Hill?
      And if they were vultures?
And if an aberrant shovel, and no one's intention,

cracked Remus in the head?
The outlines, brilliant without depth, cannot be judged,
> yet each in his heart may believe that the darker half,
> the slain shadow, would have been the better king.

The city that wasn't! Specter in the alley,
> lantern's inversion! Pavor nocturnus! Remus!
> Lemurs! Larvae! Rise trembling at midnight,
>> cast bean-pods over your shoulder

> HAEC EGO MITTO

HIS (inquit) REDIMO MEQVE MEOSQVE FABIS

VII

Rape and murder have their hour,
> but it is best when they are ended;
best when they fold under Romulus like a cloak,
> smoothed to regalia and tame.

Ten curiae per tribum, ten gentes per curiam.
> A hundred-year truce binds the Etruscans of Veii.
Three thousand infantry to each legion.
> Three hundred horse in the guard.

The Aventine Hill, lost city of Remus,
> shrinks in its new-built wall.
The boys toss javelins in the forum.

The Sabine women are happy at their looms.

VIII

He has dressed in Scarlet with a purple-bordered Robe!
He gives Audience on a Couch of State!
There go before him others with Staves and leather Thongs,
    to bind on the moment whomever he commands!

    Insignibvs Virtvtibvs Eorvm Domi Forisqve S P Q R

    Romvlvs makes sacrifice at the temple of Vulcan
(man most religious, he has decreed lustrations,
    sacred fires)
    and the Senate of Rome murmurs at his back:
neither are the Patricians any longer admitted to State affairs
    only is the Name and Title left them
they convene in Council rather for Fashion's sake than Advice
they hear in silence the King's commands, and so depart
    he of his own accord has parted among his Soldiers
        what Lands were acquired by War
    and restored the Veientes their Hostages

Midday at the hill's foot, and white stone.
To appease the fire
    (let Rome not burn)
Romulus tosses live fish into the iron hearth. Then swings in state
    to find the Senate of Rome risen around him

stares and knives

He turned, they say, as in foreknowledge
of the rising wind,
the sun darkened like blood.
He laughed in their faces. Him it convened
to be made a god.

yea, it pleases the gods
—not myself, the gods—
that I be taken upward

IX

Vivet Romvlvs
in the unbodied air, in earth's magnetic lines
each jot of force a kinglet

the walls disperse but are not unmade
new masons raise high old marbles
reshape blood and bone of Romulus

Vivet Honos Lativs Semperqve Vocabitvr
Vno Nomine Romanvm Imperivm

the sky his skull, the sea his ichor
in paths of birds his dark will
all roads conduce to his core

in pulsed harmony of milestones
the wandering tribes his errant children
of mundivorous mind

X

IVPITER OMNIPOTENS
victor's laurels
AVDACIBVS ANNVE COEPTIS
our burden

glory of Mary and the martyrs
you owe to Romulus dome and altar
furling cross of Andrew and George
the arm of Romulus holds the scourge

SAECLORVM NASCITVR ORDO
Aeneas and his gunboats
new Carthage, new Troy

children of plains and temperate waters
ships of Romulus keep your borders

ANNVIT COEPTIS

heaven's broad hand

ANNVIT COEPTIS

and a curse on that poet
whose words Romulus' arm prolongs

Paul Kerschen

ANNVIT COEPTIS

a curse on that poet
who speaks but with mouth and tongue of ROMVLVS

THOTH

1

a, *indef. art.* The beginning of everything. Unlike *the*, which introduces only some stale thing we've already met, *a* picks out new promises. As in Pound: "Petals on a wet, black bough." *The* black bough would have indicated something in the outer world. But *a* black bough appears in the mind from nowhere, as a gift of grace. And who can compel the gift? And how long till the gift comes? A drawer of old verse growls at the bottom of my file cabinet, and nowhere in it is anything to equal Pound's petals.

aa, *n.* To say that life is hard is to say something like this: at the beginning it flows like magma, hot and viscous, engulfing all it touches in the blazing stream; then one morning you wake to find it hardened in a stony heap around you, rough and pitted and alien. If you touch it you'll scrape your knuckles. If you try to walk you'll fall and skin your knees. It's not impossible that magma still runs under the surface—here and there you feel a ghost of old heat—but you can't know for sure, and life will be very different from now on.

aardvark, *n.* A toothless clown. Ears, snout, sticky tongue, all made for ridicule. Take the stage, aardvark! Dig for ants, make us laugh! If only I'd been born with that face—how many aardvarks I've seen triumph in life.

aardwolf, *n*. But some clowns do have teeth. And the ants don't find the aardvark funny at all.

aback, *adv*. A comfort. Time present beats at your sails, spins you in eddies—time past you might understand. My childhood was terribly spoiled. Young adulthood dragged me around American highways like a cargo trailer, collecting diplomas on my wall and notches in my heart. For twenty-five years I've lived in San Francisco, a congenial city where each afternoon the past condenses in white tendrils over the water, blows inland and wraps the streets in nebulous layers. The sun fizzles into a sourceless gray glow, and the storefronts and houses take on the watery scent of absent things. Of the friendships I've made here, the most lasting has been with N., a painter my own age, onetime political radical, now assistant at an interior design shop, expert on early music and Italian wines, still a handsome man even with crow's feet and hair waned to a crescent over his nape. He and I were lovers once, briefly, in a decade when nobody distinguished much between lovers and the rest of the world. That we've remained friends is a credit to his generosity and tact, not mine. Age has given us habits. Once or twice a month we meet at a trattoria tucked around the corner from Mission Street, order pastas and wine and espresso and talk about the past. We used to meet in his studio; I'd read him my poems, which were trying to marry Hopkins to Bashō, and he'd show me his canvases of white filigree—always the same thin line, with razor-crisp edges—

looped over color fields. Now he doesn't paint, and I don't write, and we look aback.

abacus, *n*. It happened about fifteen years ago. Computer firms were sprouting like mushrooms over the city, I took a job with one of them, and it's as if that day I wandered into an infinite spreadsheet with each blank cell so like its neighbor that I immediately lost my path. But all this time some register in me must have been counting the debt, because last night I woke in the dark, sat up and shouted: fifty thousand words, twenty-five words a day, that's only five years! I cried it aloud, I swear. I think I have that long. Samuel Johnson took nine years for his *English Dictionary*, but that was a harder job. He had to collect examples from the world's speech. I intend to sing only myself.

<A portion of the file could not be recovered.>

acquire, *v*. A verb that takes only certain objects: wealth, data, inventory, tastes, languages, corporations, colonies, immunodeficiency syndrome. They say it's no longer a death sentence. Which means it's only like the death sentence everyone shares—no panic, no real pity, only an understanding that you can't plan your life into eternity. Who knows where the poison gift came from. (You can infer, you can infer all the wakeful night, it goes nowhere.) So long as I'm not truly suffering, so long as they refill the drugs in the fridge each month, it helps cast light on what's important. Three weeks ago I had the news for certain. For the last two weeks I've written every day. I cannot say what it means to have this again.

acquit, *v.* But you infer, and the inferences lead you back to one of memory's gardens, a few nights that Cavafy might have written, half realized, distant even in the moment, green eyes—I forgive, I forgive.

<Lacuna.>

atelier, *n.* After a hundred days' work, I think the word is earned. Like everyone in San Francisco I rent for a couple hundred dollars more than I can afford, but the monthly penance gets me ten-foot ceilings, dark moldings on the doorways, a balcony with a sliver-thin view of the bay and the Oakland hills, tiled countertops and trusty plumbing and a spare room to outfit as my workshop. In here I keep a desk and bookcase; lamp, rug, querulous old PC; a decanter of Scotch I won't apologize for. I've hung up places where the eye can wander in midsentence—framed lithographs, a painting of N.'s—but more and more my gaze is turning to a mark I've noticed on the opposite wall, a faint oval shape that puts me in mind of Virginia Woolf's short story. Of course Woolf didn't *want* to examine her mark. She loved the cloud of associations—the mystery of life; the inaccuracy of thought!

atemporal, *adj.* It's an egg, is what it is. Just the size and shape of a chicken's egg, perhaps a touch elongated, speckled a dried-blood ochre. It reminds me of those wall paintings in Egyptian tombs, loaded with goods for the afterlife. I mean the sturdiest paintings, those sculpted in relief, because in certain lights my mark, like Woolf's, seems actually to project from the wall.

athanasy, *n.* Dinner last night with N. Usually the trattoria lets him uncork something from his own collection, but last night's Greek bottle was too much for our waiter. What did you bring in here, he cried, the horrible grapes that grow on those islands, they're only good for vinegar. N. threw back some connoisseur's talk about xynomavro, but all evening the waiter made faces at us, even after we'd killed the bottle and I grew eloquent on the *athanatoi theoi*. The Greek gods are deathless, I declared, only because Homer himself is deathless; and N. smiled and said, well, whatever Homer was. The oral tradition personified? A Sicilian woman? That's the point, I said, we don't know, the worker became the work, refined himself out of existence, passed into eternity. N. lifted his silver brows—he does a particular ironic thing with those brows, stretching the crow's feet around his kindly blue eyes—and said, oh, eternity. A fine and private place, but none, I think, do there embrace. Doesn't it bother you, I asked, that you don't paint any more? He looked out the window and I felt ashamed. I'd been about to announce my new work. But even with half a bottle of xynomavro in me, I knew it would be unkind.

athanor, *n.* The more I write, the more distinctly the egg appears on my wall. It's not a tomb painting, I've decided, it's a portent of life. The Easter resurrection, the furnace incubating the philosopher's stone—and as I type this, the egg drops from the wall, hits the rug and rests there, solid and whole.

atheism, *n.* My first thought was to eat it. Weird dream-ideas barged into my head: I have a sickness, I need strong medicine. I crouched over it, touched the brittle surface—it's warm. What to do? It feels like theft, like a policeman should be coming up the stairs. I cupped it in my palms, stared into the slight oval cavity in the wall, a kind of navel: finally I set it under the desk lamp. It will get heat there. And if it's no theft at all, but a gift? From whom—the gods? What would that mean?

<Lacuna.>

attend, *v.* Latin: to stretch the soul. All night, and all day, and all night again I've kept the lamp lit. This morning there was a small hole in the shell; now it's begun to crack, rocking back and forth and making little sharp noises. Several times I've wanted to help it along with a pencil, but I hold back, I think it needs to happen without me.

<Lacuna.>

augury, *n.* Three days since it dropped from the wall, and the gift is out: no Easter chick, no scaled monster, just a dirty white duckling, half blind and trembling in the lamplight, with stubs for wings and a neck like a rubber band. And maybe that's what a hatchling duck should be. But the noise it makes! It hasn't stopped since I came home; it quivers and cries, not loud but expressing the most awful want, shaking the air like a violin string, piercing the ceilings and floors, striking everyone in the building with a dreadful reminder of the needy things they've spurned in their lives. What have I got for food? I bring it a water dish, whatever ridiculous things I have in the kitchen: milk, biscotti, strawberries, pellets torn from a bakery loaf. It ignores everything. I push a bit of strawberry flesh against its beak, it twists away and keens— want, want, want. It will burn the heart right out of me. I start to chew one of the bread pellets, remembering what mother birds do: should I swallow and cough it up? Is that possible? Someone's going to knock, the long-delayed policeman, the building manager from downstairs, the things they'll say about keeping animals in the building, unhappy animals that bring nothing but remorse, I can't go to the door, without thinking I go to my desk, open up my document, type: Three days since it dropped from the wall—and the tiny bird turns calm.

august, *adj.* And it stays calm. Huddled under the lamp, dirty down puffed out, blinking its newly opened eyes. What an idea… that it needs words? Remember what Jesus said about bread alone. But for him the word of God was *rhēma theou*, a spoken word. I don't know, I'm a ludicrous old antiquarian, but maybe, maybe here is a way forward. Twenty-three more entries tonight.

\<Lacuna.\>

azidothymidine, *n.* First thing mornings, before shower or breakfast, I go to the fridge and pull out the vial of sterile water where my prescription powder has dissolved overnight. I warm the fluid in my hand while I unwrap the syringe, lift my pajama shirt and run a cold alcohol wipe over my side, draw up the mixture with care against air bubbles, pinch a roll of fat, pierce myself and push the stuff in. And again when I come home from work. Together with the daily pills, four of one kind, six of another, it keeps the virus sleeping. Of course it can't die, it hides in the body's powerful places, where magic is strongest: the retina, the testes, the brain. But I'm getting accustomed. Tonight I broke the news to N. Oh my God, he said, how long have you known? About four months, I said. And you never, he said, I mean, I've seen you so often since then. Please, I said, I had to wait. You know me, don't you? And he said yes, of course I know you. After a while it got easier. We remembered old friends, gone many years. N. reminded me how the AZT capsules used to come printed with tiny unicorns—why unicorns, we and our dying friends would ask each other, smiling heartbroken, what kind of children are we turning into. I told N. about the different kinds of pill I'd been through, they all complicate your life in different ways, they have the silliest comic-book names, my favorite is Rescriptor. Rescriptor, said N., that would appeal to you. It blocks reverse transcriptase, I explained, which is the virus's weapon, that's how it writes its RNA back into your DNA. Everything trying to write itself forward. Is that an epigram? asked N., widening his kind eyes. Well, it's what Wilde said, I answered. Your paintings, weren't they self-portraits? I don't think so, said N. But whenever I look at those white squiggles, I said, I see your face. I have an idea. I think the dictionary should be rewritten. Or someone should write a proper commentary for it, a Talmud, with everything that dictionaries leave out. The souls of words. Because that's still the question—how a word, this impersonal thing you can copy and paste and alphabetize, how it expresses the soul. N. blinked a little and finally said, well it's a cute idea, but who'd *read* the thing? Put it to posterity, I said. Do you mean you're, said N., and I made a sphinx smile and got up for the bathroom. All the posters for these drugs show men and women in the peak of fitness, sailing, climbing mountains; but since I started them, I spend several bad hours each week on the toilet.

azimuth, *n.* It grew so fast, like a wild weed; only a couple of weeks and up went the long neck, down curved the bill into an old man's frown, out sprang soft spines and unfurled into brilliant white feathers: all except for the black tail, the bare black head. The size of a goose now—so I say, though when have I known any geese—it no longer fits on the desk and has abandoned its foster mother, the warm lamp. For a while it roosted in a corner, and when I came into the room I'd find it standing on one leg with its neck snaked against its breast, slender and bright and otherworldly. But something about the spot seemed to worry it, maybe the lowness, and lately it's taken up residence in the bookcase, where a squat row of pocket dictionaries gives it space to huddle. So far it's lived the quietest of lives. Only sometimes a jolt of electricity seems to ruffle it and it jabs its dark beak between books, turns to dig under its wing and releases scraps of floating down. There is no excrement. By now I've guessed the species, of course, and learned a few things. In Egypt they were not only sacred but useful; they ate snails and kept schistosomiasis out of the river. But this one needs only words. Then is it only the idea of an ibis? Would that make it unreal, in any important sense? Old Ulysses, plotting his audacious last voyage, picked a star to steer by and marked a point on the earth's horizon.

<Lacuna.>

bullion, *n.* Phone calls from N. pile up in my voicemail, I never call back, if I stopped to think I'd find it shameful, but I can't stop, all day at work I stack numbers in ornamental columns and when I come home it's directly to the computer and my twenty-five nightly entries. I type like an avalanche, like Sviatoslav Richter pounding the piano. If the Scotch gets into my head it floats my brain like an exotic dessert, quivering each thought like a compass needle, tuned to heaven's weather, I could never concentrate like this before, words never poured out so, how can I stop to answer the phone—this is what I try to explain to N., months too late, when we finally meet for dinner. N. makes a face like a doctor or school principal and asks how my health is. What does he think, that I'm batty with disease already? I'm fine, I say, it's not the syndrome it used to be. Tell me how you are. He shakes his head and says, I don't think you even want to know. What the hell's happened to you? And I try once again to explain the work, a dictionary written sideways, and N. waves a hand to cut me off and says, all right, all right, I'm sure it's genius, just tell me, is it safe to drink with the drugs you're on? I laugh and tell him that the drugs are supposed to keep me alive, not pack me into an early coffin. Let's order wine. Or didn't you bring something? I'm not keeping a wine collection right now, says N., and he drops the doctor face and I see the gentle sky in his eyes. You and your writing, he says, you used to get so fucking holy about it. That's the difference between you and me. I never saw it as a calling. I couldn't stand you sometimes. He's trying to make me blush, and I do, a little, but I won't argue back. Fine, I say, if you don't want to hear about it, tell me about yourself. You really want to know, says N. Yes, I say, unless you'd rather spend the evening telling me what a prick I am. I lost my job at the design shop, says N. A few months back. And maybe you've noticed there are no jobs in this town. So there's no wine collection at the moment, because there's no apartment at the moment—and then Sal the waiter, our old friend, shows up and starts to abuse us both for having been away so long. I order a huge spread of food, primi and secondi both, for N. too, who's suddenly lost the power of speech and is looking at his thumbs on the tablecloth. Well for God's sake, I say after Sal leaves, where are you staying? In the stockroom, says N. What stockroom? I ask. The stockroom at the design shop, says N. What, I say, the design shop that laid you off? Precisely, he says, you *are* a genius. Don't be snide, I say, how can you be sleeping in the stockroom when you don't even work there? N. says, if I were still *working* in the stockroom, my dear, I wouldn't *have* to sleep there, and I say, but there are places to go, you could call people, why didn't you call me? and N. says, I did call you, a number of times if you remember, but I have scruples, and I wasn't about to decant my tale of personal woe all over the voicemail of someone who can't even be bothered to call back for friendship's sake. A flush quickens his face, making him young in the half light; he stares just under my own eyes as in quarrels decades ago, when we were lovers; I want to slap those hot cheeks, grab his face and shake it; anger pulls me up like a black bubble and I make a loud, nervous laugh and say, my God, what a fucking prima donna you are, you think I'm bad? You're not sleeping in the stockroom tonight, you're coming home with me. I wouldn't do that, N. says stiffly, I wouldn't profane your hermitage, and I grab his wrist and say, I love you, you stupid old queen, now cut the shit. Sal appears with wine and crostini and zucca gialla soup, spreads everything on the tablecloth, and N. has to smile and I know all will be well, the gold of our friendship is unadulterable, old gold, pure raw essence of gold.

bullition, *n*. The things you forget. Walking N. up the stairs, I hear a faint knocking like radiator pipes or a machine in the street, no matter, we're drunk and happy and done with the world. At the dark oak frame of my beautiful high door, I juggle my keys and N. puts his hand on my shoulder and whispers, is someone *in* there? I tilt my ear to the door, and he's right, the noise is coming from inside. For a moment I can't think why. Then I say oh, and my blood starts to flow again. It's fine, I say to N., I forgot to tell you there's a bird. A bird? asks N. I'll show you, I say, swinging the door open, ready to explain, and there it is in the front entry, huge with wings fully spread, flapping around the high ceilings, shrieking and wheezing, dear God, is that really the only noise it can make, it's been silent since the day it hatched, it's awful with that beak, banging into the light fixture over and over. N. stands in the hall and stares with his mouth slack, I want to tell him this isn't usual, it's not supposed to behave like this, he shouts and a feathery wind hits my back and I fall down. It's on top of N., beating him with wild wings, what if it sticks the beak in him, is it too close for that, I stand and try to pull it off, like wrestling a cyclone, somehow we get it back in the apartment and I slam the door and we stand in the hall, scraped and breathing hard against the tumult on the other side.

bullock, *n.* I grew up in cow country. Teenaged, drunk after midnight, I'd hop fences and go walking among the herd, just to be near them. Never a thought that those tons of flesh could turn against me.

bullshit, *n., v., adj., interj.* N. turns and starts down the stairs, slowly, his arm on the rail bearing most of the load. I follow him, weak-kneed myself, saying sorry, I'm sorry, really it never does that, strangers must upset it. N. doesn't say anything until we're out the door—then in the wet, yellow-lit street he swings around and shouts, where did you *get* that thing? I didn't get it anywhere, I say, it just came. When I started writing. Came? he asks. You opened a window and it flew in? It made sense, I say. Because of the writing. That a god might come. Again N. makes the doctor's face, surely he's right to make it, I stand convicted of idiocy. He pushes his hands into his jacket, looks up at the dark window and says, I still don't understand what took you away for six months. Oh N., I plead, I thought you'd understand if anyone. I found out I was sick, I thought I should write a tragedy, don't we all feel tragic in secret, it's just that you can't build tragedies the old way, you can't point to them any more, they're like air currents, like radio, nowhere and everywhere—so I thought, the only way to write it would be to throw out words, like dust in the air, until the lines of force appeared. Like gravestone rubbings, or filings over a magnet. N. won't look at me, he keeps staring at the window, I want to tell him not to bother, it never comes to that window, it's dark inside anyway. Finally he says, how about tonight? Will you write this, too? I'm caught off guard, I don't answer, and he exclaims, you will, I knew it. Six months I don't see you, and now my shit luck, nowhere to live, your killer bird, it's all material. Go on, he says cruelly, I bet you even have a word picked out. Meekly I say: bullion. Bullion? he says. It's where I am in the dictionary, I say; but he's right, it's the worst thing yet, a valueless word, worse than valueless, it makes our lives into farce. Oh Lord. There's no explaining this, I just want to get away from him, go back to the work, to the god, maybe it's calmed down by now. Bullion, N. says again. Why not—and he spits out his suggestion. His voice is helpless as mine, it's not even a clever thing to say, he knows it's not clever, we never used to fall back on such stupid jabs. Fine, I say coldly, that's a clear position at least, and turn and go back inside.

bully, *n., v., adj.* The project was to write myself perfectly. In the process I would write the world perfectly as well. How could the world object?

bulrush, *n.* The stairs are quiet now. I find the ibis inside, roosted back in the bookcase as if it had never left. Persecutor! I shout. Punishing spirit! It blinks like any animal, and looks around at things that aren't there. It reminds me of party guests who used to stay too late, back when I gave parties, holding the cognac hostage and boring us all to tears. What can I do? I sit, squint through my wine headache at the bright computer screen, and write what I've written. The victorious ibis blinks and meditates beside me until something pricks it; then it lifts its head and starts digging its beak into the books, forcing open my tiny dictionaries and thesauri and ripping out their pages. I should do something—but no, let it be, I never open those books, it's all computers now anyway. Once the pages are loose it starts to shred them, involved as only animals get involved in things, leveraging its neck and beak to tear off strips. Its head knocks aside the gutted bindings and it heaps paper in the cleared space. We'll have a nest.

2

jynx, *n.* The company, says my supervisor, had to make some decisions it would rather have avoided. You can't imagine what I'd do to avoid carrying them out. It's like—he stops to wipe his forehead, his whole face is red and wet—let's be honest, it feels to me, having known you and everyone so long, like I have to take apart a house that I built with my own hands. That took ten years to build. Only worse, because it's a matter of dismantling, or dis—he stops, hunting the word—you know, disattaching *people*, because the lintels are people, all the, er, floorboards, the two-by-fours are people. A lot of people. I'm sorry, he says, I'm rambling, this upsets me so much. But I understand him perfectly. His glasses drop unfashionably low on his cheeks, his neck is wry, a weird gray lock curls the wrong way on his brow; this is why he is human, and really distressed, and I feel much worse for him than for myself. If we can do anything at all, he says, to make this easier, and I wish I had something to tell him, he wants it so badly. But look at me, detached as a soap bubble on the spring wind; I say thank you, you've done more than everything, I'll be just fine, never doubt it. And buoyant and rainbow-hued, I float right out the window.

ka, *n*. The Chapter of not letting the heart of a man be taken away from him. The Chapter of not letting the head of a man be cut off from him. The Chapter of making a man to return to see again his home upon earth. The Chapter of not dying a second time. I may not have mentioned that a year or more ago, ten or fifteen thousand entries back, I made a point of collecting some material on ancient Egypt. Reprints of Victorian treatises for the most part, by authors who had only just discovered the resemblance between Osiris and Christ. What can you say about the Book of the Dead, about those tomb paintings? They were meant to be immortal, and so they are, since they lack anything we recognize as life. Power they certainly have, a kind of vitality, but that's not life, it's not messy enough. The construction of profile head, squared shoulders, profile hips isn't something that a living human body can be made to do, it's only an idea of the human, and even if the written language weren't made of such pictures it would still be a kind of word. Only words are rigid enough to grasp the immortal. The ka that is the hero of the Book of the Dead is the flesh made word, and the spells that sustain it are a glass lattice hung from the night sky, a vocabulary of stars. A false door is carved in the tomb wall, a door that is a glyph of a door, and the ka steps through it to eat the inscriptions. And I'm supposed to care about a layoff? I'm not myself, I should have explained, I've stepped halfway through the door already, this is shadow and the spirit is elsewhere, writing itself new skeleton and sinew, a thought-body that will not betray it—

kabuki, *n.* K is not going to be an easy letter. So many loanwords I know nothing about. Famous for interminable death scenes, I think, worse than Italian opera.

kachina, *n.* City at dusk: what spirit moves the fog. Walking up the hill I get mist-choked and lose my breath; this is my weakest time, when floating scraps of dark swirl between my eyes and the street. Buzz in the ears—I know, much worse is coming. No one in the office guessed I was sick. Pride kept my mouth shut. At the hill's summit, woozy and flushed, I place my fingers against a wall and pull off my cap. Lady of mist, cool my scalp. I find my key, the key finds the door, I gain the stairs. My rooms are waiting for me—my balcony, as it happens, just above the moment's fog and giving onto a sad red evening of roofs and sloped clouds, antennas glinting at neglected angles, cars with lit eyes and black bodies still clear in outline. This world the only world, a painting I make for myself each moment. I watch until the red light fades; then I move back into my study to find the light switch and the colony of ibises. There must be twenty or more by now. They roost under my desk, in corners, on shelves, in the litter of destroyed books. A few eggs, a few chicks, but they all grow very fast into the same form. I can't say which was the first. Hello, friends. Let's try conclusions. I've had a few papers this afternoon—hold them up. We have here some material on the Consolidated Omnibus Budget Reconciliation Act, on the right to choose to continue group health benefits provided by your group health plan for limited periods of time under certain circumstances such as voluntary or involuntary job loss, et cetera, at a premium not to exceed 102 percent of the cost of the plan for similarly situated individuals plus 2 percent for administrative costs. While COBRA rates may seem high, you will be paying group premium rates, which are usually lower than individual rates, et cetera. Is it clear? The state—I cast some sheets across the room, clumsy sails that rattle through the air until the curved beaks snap them up—excuse me, the state has become aware of me, or might be made aware of me, as a target for assistance. What shall we call it? It is a building where we are housed, but not all have appointed rooms. It is an organism that encompasses us, but the limbs war with the head. It is a father who comes with gifts and requirements, but what a doddering Lear he is, he doesn't know his own mind, he has too many principles to follow. He knows that I am his child and mustn't suffer, but he refuses to give me anything unearned, he won't see his seed spoiled. And what a child I've been! What to do about poetry, or the sin of Sodom? He'd like to forget both, but so long as they exist he can't ignore them, not he who has made all things his business. For the first he has some use, he has to look the kings of the world in the eye, so he'll toss a few coins for public readings and inscriptions on the sidewalk. But does there have to be so *much* of it? A few poets would serve his purpose, but why all these thousands applying for grants and crowding the subway? As for the second—I toss another few sheets—it serves no purpose at all, inverted and issueless, if only he could forget it entirely. The complexity of his feelings! He is disgusted and yet he's obliged, he can't saction such inverted relations by law, yet when they breed disease he must care for the stricken. Within limits. At no unreasonable public expense. The stricken will be handled thus. At a monthly rate he will sell them piecemeal admissions to limbo, by way of syringes that have drawn up the waters of Acheron. The stricken will be permitted to remain at life's threshold, to walk with Aristotle and Ovid and other virtuous inverts, for brief spans (since they are tied to the toilet), with a black haze over the coming months and years. This arrangement will continue until they run out of money, at which point the wheel of finance will pivot beneath them and leave them hanging like bats from its underside, compounding new debts with every breath, until they expire. Alienate what you can, children. Sell what is sellable. An apartment with a writing studio, a colony of unearthly birds—if you wish your father's protection, shed these burdens. This much suffices: an efficiency room with adjoining water closet, a couch that nightly becomes a bed, alley view, electric range, miniature fridge stocked with medicine and soft food. That is the offer! I fling the last pages, they rattle aloft, the birds snap them up, they've already begun to rip the sheets into pieces, their appetite for paper has no end. This is making fine theater. The alternative, friends and persecutors, awful gods, is simple. To stay and refuse. To send back the syringes. To empty my husk of life. Shall I? What oratory. Will you take me entire? They twist their necks, they shred, they nod. White wings open from their bodies, extend glories of pinion feathers, refold. None to see but I. None to record but I. I'll keep you, awful gods, and you me.

kaddish, *n.* Rap at the front door: sharp, commanding, three times. Was I speaking out loud? Shouting? A neighbor, landlord? I ease out of the sanctum, shut the ibises inside and tiptoe to the door. Through the peephole I see only stairs, the brown hall. My hand hesitates at the bolt—it was so loud, the door's never been struck like that. I draw it open. Outside is the neutrality of a shared hallway: my neighbor's shut door, scuffed floorboards, the filament glowing orange in a glass sconce. Air like still water. No presence but I. For years I've climbed these steps, each day made them more my own, and in a moment all that history is wiped away. Something has touched them, they don't know me. I push the door slowly to, not wanting to provoke the alien hall; then the knock comes again, three times, farther now, I think from the bottom of the stairwell. An outer door stands there, with three frosted panes the color of night. They were not built to reveal.

kairos, *n.* Down the stairs, I repeat my shy dance: creeping steps, eye to the mail slot. Outside is dull dusk, objects that seem drawn in charcoal and a pale dog standing in a puddle. Must I open? As my worn soles touch the sidewalk I feel a moment's boldness: what could this empty street want from me? What is it entitled to ask? But the dog has its eye on me, a pale blotch in bad light, and I'm not sure it's a dog at all. It's more like a miniature wolf, very thin under a sand-colored pelt, its eyes glinting gold under the street lamp. A long grin runs up its muzzle. Its legs are all bone. I am meant to follow.

kaka, *n.* A parrot.

kakapo, *n.* I said a parrot, in peril. Extinction. I'm sorry, what am I doing? Saying this? As if writing and acting were taking place at the same time, as if the world were parroting my own words back at me. I imagine things before I see them. The small wolf-dog jogs ahead on starved legs, leading me toward the palms and broad pavement of Dolores Street, and I think: these streets must be empty. And so they are. The streetlights should recede, the fog should clear—and heaven sparkles white and blue as only in the deepest country, ready to spill stars onto my head. We have been speaking of death, we need an emblem, and in the form of the old mission, under the floodlit terrace and white wall, I discover a dark gateway, a gap in the adobe, that I had never noticed before. A harsh grinding sound carries down the street, repeating every few seconds. The wolf-dog slows and pads into the shadow. I follow and find a mesh fence split by a jagged rent my own height. I duck and step through into a courtyard of tombstones lit by starlight. Between the graves are thick trunks of palms, heavier trees with weeping branches, funeral statues with spread wings. Grass and vines run thick on the ground. At the far wall stands a man in rolled-up shirtsleeves, scraping at a headstone.

kaleidograph, *n.* He's a large fellow, with broad shoulders and forearms emerging lean from his rolled cuffs. His shape is wonderfully clear in the faint light, but he wears dark glasses and his head is shaved so that his age is hard to fix. His shirt and slacks are well cut—I have an eye for it. The tombstone lies between him and me, and it's hard to be sure what he is doing, but he seems to be working some kind of metal rasp over the grave marker's face, with his mouth set tight, either in effort or in displeasure at the screech he's making. He pays no mind to my approach, and it seems that his task must have fully possessed him; but when I clear my throat he interrupts in a loud voice, pitched high for such a large man, without looking up and without ceasing to scrape.

kaleidophone, *n.* There's no room in this city, he says. We built it on a rock in the middle of the water, and look at us now: we've run out of space. Ever try to park a car in the financial district? That's the way of everything. Too many units, not enough slots. Blind robbery on office leases. Warehouses. My condo. Even after you're dead: do you know this is the only cemetery inside the city limits? There's nowhere else to be buried. And this place filled up a century ago. I have to make some room. And he sets his mouth and keeps scraping—but whose name is he grinding away? I've been trying, while he speaks, to move to his side of the headstone, but he seems to understand what I'm doing and keeps placing his broad back between me and it. Now as I come very close, he moves his whole form to block me and I see the flash of a naked knife at his side, stuck crudely under his glossy belt.

kaleidoscope, *n.* You see! he barks. You made me show it before it was time. I want to follow an order here. For my own sake, and for my wife's. Now I see the woman, standing farther back against the wall. I must have taken her for a grave statue. Her face is lowered, hidden in dark hair, and she has wrapped her arms tight to herself. Instantly I feel that she must be an ally, that together she and I might bring the man to his senses. But she makes no response when I extend my hand,

and the man begins to scrape more violently still, grumbling: Haven't I got the right to choose our deaths? If a man can't choose the face he's born with, can't force his way in the world, can't set the hour of his ruin, shouldn't he have this much to trust in?

kalpa, *n.* Enough! I shout. If I were bolder, I would tear the rasp from his hand. Why all this opera? I'm sure it's entertaining, but it doesn't mean anything, not unless you're planning to scratch it all into that headstone. Surely you don't think you'll carry it beyond the grave? If we believed in an afterworld, if we trusted that ghosts could walk, that would be one thing. But you know what's waiting for you! I point to the thin, grinning wolf-dog, which has seated itself beside the headstone and watches us with bright golden eyes. In that mouth, I say, your mortal remains will perish. As for the immortal, there will nothing but the words spoken of you—if there are to be any words at all. Without a chronicle you're nothing.

kamikaze, *n.* I suppose *you're* offering to chronicle me, he says. You want to hear about my rise and fall, is that it? To record my ruin? He barks a laugh. You must have a nose for these things. I was an investment banker.

kangaroo, *n.* He stops his scraping, lays his rasp on the stone and draws himself upright. Now he seems even larger but ungainly, his empty hands hanging like useless forepaws. It's all gone, he says. I used to think I was chosen. I saw transactions the way other people see traffic signals. Most of them warned me away, red, red, red; but every twentieth light would come up green. That was my call. I would pour in my millions. It upsets your feeling of gravity, pouring away millions of dollars in a morning. Those eight figures that were your foundation no longer support you, the balance drops out of your inner ear, you tumble free in the wind. Yet after each of these leaps, I would land on a higher eminence than before—until the day that I didn't, when I failed to find my feet. The green light turned red before I could reach it, and as I tumbled into the wind's underside, I wondered—suppose I'd been colorblind all along? If this was the point to which all those green lights had led, how could I know what their true color had been? What thing were they tied to? Tell me, he demands, and pulls the dark glasses from his face; his brows are thick and white, his pale eyes set in folds of skin, he's much older than I thought. Tell me, does the word *abacus* mean anything to you?

kanji, *n*. Abacus! I cry. Why, every job I've ever had has asked me to be an abacus. I mean a dead brain, a row of counters for someone else to manipulate. I understand, he says; that's the view from the bottom of the office. Now let me explain the view from the top. These counters I used to manipulate—which, as you say, include the brains of other men—obey a clear logic among themselves. Five beads on one string will always equal one bead on the next. But what links these counters to the world? What was I moving other than placeholders, null values? This was my blindness, and not only mine. Abstraction brought down our whole economy. If it had been a matter of work, real work like I'm doing on this stone—and he takes up the rasp again—that would have been different. But these were weightless, derivatives of derivatives, ghost transactions. We should never have started to print paper money. Gold and silver, a cap on usury, that would have saved us. And I'll tell you something: this is why China is going to take over the world. Because they were never infected by the virus of abstraction. Because they have a picture language where words are things. That simple fact contains the sum of their cultural wisdom. The word *crisis*, for them, is an opportunity—or it's that danger is opportunity, crisis plus opportunity equals—no, he muttered, resuming his scraping with a scowl, how does it go?

kaon, *n.* It's not true, says the woman. Her voice has a strange quality, and as she lifts her head I see that her features are Asian. Her face is round and cold in the starlight, and her hair is streaked gray; she too is older than I thought. There is a dark bundle in her wrapped arms. He doesn't understand any language, she says with a strong accent, not even his own. But I had to learn it. I came to this city, and I worked in the law. For years I was only a typing machine. But after typing millions of other people's words I realized something: that a word is not a picture. It shows nothing. A word is a tool, and when you put your hand to the word it becomes a lever to set the world in motion, or else to halt it. When I understood this, I was finished as a typing machine, and instead of carrying the words of others I began to use my own. I was cruel. To my parents across the ocean I used such words as can't be forgiven. I've led an angry life, and I've broken many bonds. But I've come out with knowledge. He keeps that knife in his belt and imagines it's a secret from me. But I know a word that, if I chose to speak it, would cut him down where he stands.

karaoke, *n.* She sets her face hard, as if turning back into a funeral statue, and I realize that she and the man both are speaking as the dead speak. For the dead too are like written words; they have their single story, with beginning and end linked into a single shape, and they can't be brought to tell another. Still we want to turn them aside, to break the barrier of accomplished facts, as when in the dark movie theater we cry out to the heroine—don't open the door!—expecting that she might turn her face to us—

karate, *n.* Stop this, I plead. Surely neither of you means what you're saying. I understand, the world is emptier than you once thought, you yourselves are worse than you once thought—believe me, I understand very well. Mourn if you have to; but why die for it? Once you've scraped the name from that stone, you'll pull out the knife and make it an altar: is that the idea? It can't be the thing you want. Not with a child! For I have finally made out the bundle in the woman's arms: the dark cloth has fallen back and the infant's head seems to float free in its folds, a tiny hovering planet with dark eyes. Is it afraid? I've never spent time around infants. Do they have minds? Is there anything in there but a buzz? This one isn't laughing or crying, it only stares with those great dark orbs—and it seems, though perhaps all is illusion, that its gaze has fixed on the grinning dog at the headstone. I have a terrible sense that this child knows more than I ever will, that in its empty head is a kind of second sight, the way animals can sense earthquakes ahead of time, and that without knowledge of past or future it is already living through its own death. The thought is too cruel to bear. Spare the child! I beg, and stretch out my empty hands.

karyotype, *n.* The man shakes his head and says: the child goes with us. Otherwise it would propagate our forms.

113

kasbah, *n.* And what of it! I say. Do you have the right to halt them? You, I ask the woman, did you give him that right?

katabasis, *n.* She looks away and draws the cloth over the child's eyes so that only the tiny mouth and chin are visible, white and dry. The shame of it, says the man. After all I've been through, I want only to end the shame. Let the jackals carry it off. He stretches a hand to the canine form; it raises its muzzle and sniffs.

katana, *n.* Let me have him! I reach forward, the man draws his knife; falling back toward the child, I get my first glimpse of the headstone's face and see that it has been scraped wholly smooth. A white light flashes behind the mesh fence: the moon must be rising. My breath is short, yellow and black buzz films over my eyes.

katharevousa, *n.* I hold my arms before me, levers poised for battle, ready to spill blood, to save anyone who can be saved. To keep the child from the jackal—unless the jackal is not meant to destroy the child? Unless the jackal is to take it and raise it, as one of its own brood?

katun, *n.* How long to wait for the blow. How long we have been poised here, all alike, figures in the churchyard—

katzenjammer, *n.* I am finished.

3

Unobjectionable. Unobligatory. Unobliging.

If you want to reveal the weakness of your eyes, simply turn them to the clear sky. Against that blank blue you'll discover all the barriers that usually hide among the world's forms: the tumbling black worms, the television buzz. This mess is inside you. You can't get around it.

Unobliterated. Unobscured. Unobservable.

The sunlight is irregular, it keeps disappearing, but after a few minutes it is sure to return. Each time it turns the grass unbearably bright. Each time my mind follows, kindling painful thoughts that I can't control and didn't ask for: bits of rhyming nonsense, a train station where I was once stranded for two hours, an unkind thing said to me ten years ago. What kind of creatures are we that confound the laws of motion, that once at rest won't stay that way?

Unobstructed. Unobtainable. Unobtrusive. Unoffered.

To be a bird, or a cloud. A cloud and bird, the grass, a tree—

Unopenable. I'm going to call an ambulance.

Can you sit up? Easy. We're calling an ambulance. Do you understand? Unopened.

Warmth at my temple: someone's hand. I could swoon with comfort. I know the voice, the kind eyes.

Unoperative.

N. speaks my name. Lifting my tongue feels like reaching for something across a table. There is a handful of breath in me. Unopportune.

Did you say something? he asks. To someone behind him, a tall shadow, he says, did you catch that? I feel there's a joke somewhere in this, and reach for that faint flicker under the pain. Try to grin. Unorganized. Unorganized? says N., and the shadow says, yes, I think it was unorganized. Hm, says N., and then, should we move him? I don't know, says the shadow, I don't think we're supposed to. Oh fuck *supposed,* says N., it's humiliating to have him out on the sidewalk. He repeats my name and says, do you have your keys? Do you still keep them in your front pocket? His hand is in my clothes, it makes a fist and withdraws. Easy. Now lift. Suddenly hands are all around me, there seem to be six or eight of them, each transmits a bit of strength, how good to be moved through space. My weight tilts. Shapes pass my head. The hall sconce I recognize, with its bright filament: my own door. Once we are inside I seem to wake from a dream; the weaker tendrils of thought, without objects to attach to, thin and disperse, and the stronger knit themselves into a picture. I have been put on my sofa, under the friendly mustard-colored wall and Japanese print. N. sits nervously in the visitor's chair, and it seems I ought to be hosting him; also, I suppose, the dark-haired man behind him, who has set his hand on the chair's back. How long since anyone's been in here? I can't see the mess around me, but I imagine dust, a ruined city of books, who knows what in the kitchen and bathroom. I hope there's no smell.

You are my good knights, I say, and my heart takes a scary gallop. The room starts to swing, as if it's hanging by a string and is about to fall off, but I master my gaze and fix it on the dark-haired man. You, I say, I don't know.

Francis, N. says quickly, as if discharging an obligation. My husband.

The word wraps around the two of them. But it doesn't stick to N. It's meant for this Francis, who actually looks like a husband: sweater, haircut, thin-rimmed glasses, the back of my guest chair under his suntanned hand, which, yes, has got a ring on it. And a graciousness in his speech that seems to come out of another decade; he is saying something on the order of, N. has told me a lot about you. Is he really saying that?

When? I ask, how long? and N. says, just a few months. Is it apology or pride in his voice? We beat Prop 8 by a week. No, I say, how long since I've seen you? Oh, he says, I'm not sure. February? March? Maybe—maybe close to a year. It's terrible, he says, you lose people, especially in this city, I don't know why it happens. If we hadn't seen you on the sidewalk. How are you doing? How do you feel? I don't know, I say. Do you remember what happened? I remember things, but they're subjective. You have to plot them against me. Stop, he says, you don't have to remember anything, the ambulance is coming.

In trying to talk, I've become aware that something else is in the room, some kind of animal that is keeping near to Francis and near to the floor. It's a devourer, I think, what have they smuggled in here; and though lifting my head seems impossible, I manage a slight roll on the sofa. A child is sitting on my floorboards, beside Francis's shoes and neat cuffs. He rocks back and forth in a sideways ball cap, with monkey hands splayed on his knees. This is Larry, says N.

Larry. Hello, Larry. What does one say?

He doesn't talk much, says Francis with a fond smile; and N. breaks in, he's just come to us lately. From Cambodia. I am completely ignorant of what I ought to be saying. So Larry, I say, isn't the name he came in with; and N. says quietly, we don't know what name he came in with. It doesn't matter. We'll give him a good life.

Larry's life, N.'s life, my life. Which is good? Quite suddenly I am in Larry's mind twenty years hence, groping backward to this moment by the dusty light of first memory, when I stood apart from words, one day taken up a staircase into a dark and cluttered room where an old man lay helpless on a sofa, my fear of being watched, my fear of the old man, no place to flee.

When the ambulance gets here, I say, is it taking me to an awful home? No, says N., of course not, the emergency room. But once the emergency is over, I say, then the awful home. Yes? They won't let me stay and work.

Work! exclaims Francis, I wouldn't say you have to worry about work right now. He's fatherly as well, with a gentle trick of assertion that seems to cast him as the only adult in the room. You don't understand, I say. I'm too tired to explain. N. understands. You remember, in there. I indicate—not even nodding, with a mere glance—the shut door of my study.

N. follows my look. The door is mute; this place is the quietest in the world. Cars pass, faint, blocks away. N. says, is it still—and I say, not it: they. Ah, he says, starting to fret; and I tell him, I think you're all right. He was never slow to take hints. Francis, he says, maybe you should watch for the ambulance on the street. Take Larry down with you. No, I say, Larry can stay. In fact he should stay. He should see. Francis is making a dubious face, still playing the lone adult, but I suppose that's the only part he can play, my willfulness is forcing it on him. Anyhow he won't contradict me in my home. He says that he'll be right downstairs. Oh, N.! Why didn't you marry someone more like yourself? Why not someone I could love?

You're unsympathetic, N. says as soon as he's gone. I suppose he strikes you as a caricature. You might try to look around it. Ha, I say, are you going to lecture a dying man? I'll pretend you didn't say that, says N., and anyway I don't think you are dying. You've only been taking unbelievably poor care of yourself. I know you. You decide it's too much trouble to eat, or to take your medicine, and then it's not your fault when your apartment goes to pieces and you start passing out on the sidewalk. It's forced on you: is that what you think?

It's not so simple, I say weakly. But let's not argue, N.—don't you want to see what's inside? N. twists his long neck to regard the door and asks, is it safe? It must be, I say. N. rests a light hand on the child's shoulder. Come, Larry, he says, my friend has something to show you. Larry's black eyes turn up to him, a face that seems made of wet clay, and he lifts his arms to N. as N. bends to help me from the couch, and we all rise together, the child and I each on one of N.'s hands, weak-limbed and at gravity's mercy. My body is a toy, a heap of spindles that won't arrange; but together the three of us cross the room to the study door, which I have the honor of grasping—N. is so nervous—and opening onto the heart of the sun. It hangs framed in the window, as if just past the panes, and pours its white and gold aspect on the resplendent litter of the room. Shredded paper drowns the desk and bookcase; there is N.'s painting, richer in hue than ever before, and everywhere the brilliant ibises, roosted on the furniture, in corners and on the sill, bowing dark heads as if in expectation. Are they adoring the sun? No. Their eyes are shut. They have all shut their eyes and pulled their heads to their breasts, and they make no motion—only the faint, perhaps imaginary, rise and fall of sleeping breath. We enter. Again I see through Larry's wide eyes, as in memory, a brilliant room of shreds and white birds, a faint smell as of something laundered, the gutted spines of hardbacks. Gently I give up my body and drop to my knees, then to my side in the bed of paper, with warm birds all around; and N. is over me with a hand on my shoulder, saying not here, get up. It's all right, I say, I can rest here. It seems that this room really is the sole place where rest is permitted, where the mind's circuit could find its halt. I shut my eyes onto a blaze of red blood. I can hear N.'s cautious rustle around the room, whispering something; finally he asks, you've been writing here? All this time? Yes. Your dictionary? Yes. And is it done? But the question doesn't seem to have an answer. Through the middle of the alphabet my memory is good. After that less is clear. You can go to the computer, everything's there. Rustle of N. moving toward my desk, the sliding chair. The computer is already switched on, I can hear the fan. Keystrokes. It's giving me a warning, says N. A pause. There's a problem with the hard disk. Do you know about this? I can't remember. I don't know when I last typed anything. Well, did you at least back it up? I can't say. For the love of God, he exclaims, really angry, I thought you worked with these things, I thought you understood them. I can't even see anything on the screen. You stupid—he slams something on the desk—you threw out everything for this? N., it's all right, it doesn't matter. It damn well had better matter, he says, if it's all you have to show, but I shake my head in the paper nest, no, no. Suppose nothing is lost. Suppose everything is written in heaven. In heaven? Yes, everything. Even now. You know what I suppose, he says; then stands abruptly, and hurries from the desk. Oh no, Larry, it's all right. Honey, nobody's fighting. Look at the birds. Aren't they beautiful? And we are silent as the birds. I shut my eyes tighter, curl into myself. My shoulder is touched. Do you see this? N. whispers. I let the room back into my eyes. Sunlight on the ceiling, the birds' black heads, now very close above me. Their shut eyelids gleam like prisms. I look from one to another; I look to N., to Larry, and back again. Clear droplets are welling from the birds' shut eyes, sliding over the bare skin of their heads and down their curved beaks. A new smell has come up, medicinal or liquorous, the tincture of some flower. Can birds do this? asks N. I have no answer. What's happening? An ending. What's the last word? The last? says N. Yes, where do they stop? There used to be a dictionary in here. Some of it might be left. I wave toward my memory and N. follows, wrestles from the floor the torn blue binding of the compact *Oxford English Dictionary*, a great downed albatross with a few leaves still drooping from its spine. Here. Yes. There's some left at the end. But I can't read it. There used to be a magnifying glass. Well, there isn't one now. Then look closer. He brings a crumpled sheet to his eyes, smooths it against the binding and turns it to the sun's full blaze. Zymurgy, he murmurs. Yes, fermentation. Is that the last? No. Zythum. What is it? Unknown origin. Hellenistic Greek, Egypt. A beverage. Malt, barley. For the better avoidance and purging out of the digested venom, give the party garlic beaten with zythum, until he vomit. That's all? Meaning what? A drink. Sustenance. Purification. The tomb paintings that nourished the ka. But why here? For an ending. Has it come? Is the word made matter? It is. Why? As a passage. To taste. Will the birds grant it? They grant all ideas, they themselves are ideas, you too are idea and inviolable. They drop their heads. It is easy. But I can barely lift my own. Don't hate your body. It served you. Tongue out. Yes. To the point of the beak. Conveyance of light. I am not afraid. Once I was young, my body was beautiful; I remember how it wore its slimness, how its legs turned in the mirror. That was I. Strange. And now: strange. I am being told a story about sirens and feet on the stairs, but I'm drowsy, I won't hear the ending. You know the rest. Then it's well. Light and blood in the eyelids. It's well. A child loved what it knew. And from there.

TLALOC

A man works in the Republic. He suffers. The interstate cuts the desert like the dream of a ruler, and half a mile away a dirt road crosses a gully into an orchard's metal fence. Past the trees, the sleeping trailers for the season's workers pour heat from their roofs and perturb the mountains.

The trees are staggered in straight rows, and every step through the orchard opens new views of avenues between them. They are copies: each splits branches from its body in the same pattern. For the man on the ladder each tree is a half hour and three boxes of oranges, and when he enters the tree he is always entering the same world, leafy and yellow, the size of a room, always with the same branch at his left foot and L-shaped crook at his hip. Reaching in leather gloves, he takes not oranges but images of oranges; they break from their stems and drop to the box at his feet having touched nothing but his eyes. After an hour his mouth dries and his back and wrists cry murder. A hand in the sky wipes out the clouds and spreads the white sun everywhere, making all things enemies.

The others want to take his hat away. When the tamale truck drives up the road they all drop out of their trees and race each other, without breaking into a run, up the orchard's avenues. In the crush at the truck's rear, around the tamale woman with her dog and coffee cans packed with hot husks, the others grin at him under their mustaches, jerk their heads up and reach out to bat his straw brim. They have hats of their own, or could get them; that isn't the point. They speak with desert accents and he doesn't. His home is green.

Evenings everyone goes into the town across the interstate and drinks what he can. A burlap awning makes a trailer into a cantina; pity the benches at the doorstep, the boy who serves cans from an ice bucket. A man called Jackrabbit sits apart from the others: no rabbit ears and no rabbit teeth, but a whisper of the animal in his cheeks and hunched shoulders. He is older than most and has no friends among the workers. His pinched voice shares an accent with the man from the green country, and the man hates him for it. The town has a few young women who don't come to the cantina but stand across the street in jeans and thong sandals, watching. After his beers the man crosses the street: what an evening is open to his senses! The sun is gone but a track of burning clouds is seared behind it, and the stars shy away for fear of being caught in the blaze. Black beetles inch over the gravel, called by floodlamps, wandering centers to the miles of shadowland. The miles! The terrible clear air, bringing all distances to the eye's surface—the inalterable rocks!

"I come from a volcano," he tells the young woman in the street. "In the morning its slope was green over the earth. But in the evening it was covered with clouds, we saw nothing, and we measured distance with our limbs."

In her dark room he pulls the thong sandals from between her toes and holds her bare feet in his hands. This has happened before and has never happened before, they were not meant to suffer, they shine steady and low like candles in hushed air, the earth smiles at them through the house's foundation. In a midnight that blazes like noon they walk into the kitchen wearing nothing but blankets over their shoulders and find her mother wide awake, making coffee and tortilla soup. She sits him at the table blotched with old varnish and candle-wax and serves the meal with a command in her plump smile: she will feed him from now on.

Without telling his crew leader, he gives up his bunk in the sweat-smelling trailer. Now the others see him at dawn walking in from town and throwing his long shadow before him. They stop batting at his hat. He hasn't become their friend, but it is now at Jackrabbit and his tiny hunched shoulders that the crowd points its teeth. If Jackrabbit would only look up, they might be content to glare at him, but since he keeps his eyes to the ground, they take turns sticking their boots between his legs and making him stumble. When the man finds Jackrabbit before him, he tries a small shove and immediately takes fright: what if he turns around, his face will call judgment on me. But no one turns to look at him, not Jackrabbit and not the others. He might as well have shoved at the sky. He sets his teeth and a satisfying contempt comes to bathe his heart, lifting it up in its pillar of blood.

In his new home he eats himself into bliss. Everything is warm and wet: coffee, tomato sauce, chicken broth, endless glass jars of water from the town's tower. He and his woman swell out with joy and more—she tells him she's to be a little mother. Is she sure? A drop of ink strikes the center of his happiness, bleeds out from the core. This has never happened before and it's happened before, there's a little mother back in the green country, with children that fell like laughing stars from heaven, laughing and hungry—this is why he spends his days reaching for oranges and never touching their skins. He thought he'd made peace with all things but it was only a truce, the walls and bedposts and window frame all glare at him as enemies, he has to hit them, he hits her, she hits him back.

"You can't kill him," she shouts, "only God can kill him!"

What does that mean? Which of them does God have it in for? Her mother comes into the room, crying: I gave you coffee and water, coffee and water! They both slap at his body but can't drive him out, his feet are bolts in the floor, but as long as he stands there he'll only hear the same thing, coffee and water, so he quits the room and house and goes errant into the night, out to the interstate, where trucks flash like dragons.

At the orchard he finds his old bunk taken and darkness in every trailer, full of men who threaten him with their sleeping breath. He falls asleep outdoors on the gravel. The sun wakes him in yesterday's clothes, thirstier than ever before in his life. He gulps from the wash faucet behind the trailers and the water drops in his stomach without soothing his throat. The sheet-metal sky! When does it ever rain here? All morning he thinks of his cloudy home and feels its dew pricking his eyes, climbs into the yellow branches and sees the oranges hanging luminous under their leaves. His throat aches and aches. His dry glove takes an orange; there is another world, a heaven of rain, just under the peel. His teeth rip in. Tart oil kisses him, his tongue weeps, he takes the warm pulp in his mouth and a voice calls from below. The crew leader, a sharp-faced desert man, is squinting up at him from the bottom of the ladder.

"Spit it out," says the crew leader.

World in suspension. He stands on the ladder, juice in his mouth, far from earth.

"That's a unit out of your box and fifteen minutes docked," says the crew leader. "Spit it out."

The man looks down. His mouth closes on itself and he swallows.

The crew leader starts to yell. He shakes the ladder as if to drop him from the tree—you're off the job, off the site, I can call the immigration cops, get you kicked out of the Republic, send you back where you came from—and the man nearly strikes him in the head as he comes rattling down the ladder, shouting fine, send me back, these terrible people, this nightmare desert, send me home.

"Those are the company's gloves," says the crew leader, "give them back."

He gives up the gloves. The crew leader grabs both by the wrists and flaps them against each other in idiot applause, then reaches out and slaps them over the man's shoulders. The man jerks back and the crew leader follows, chasing him down the avenue with the empty gloves flapping at his back, until he is driven from the orchard.

During the day the cantina's door is shut, its awning is rolled up and it is only a trailer and some benches declaring their shapes in the sun. The man knocks on the door. He walks around to the dark mirror of the window and knocks again until the boy appears on the steps.

"I want to drink," says the man.

The boy looks unsure. "I'll ask them inside," he says. "It might cost extra."

"My money is in a pair of pants I don't have," says the man, "in a house in back of here. I was saving it to send home."

The boy shrugs. "So save it to send home."

"No," says the man, "I want to drink it. Can't you give me credit, until I get my clothes back?"

The boy disappears. After a short while he comes back, looking unhappy, and rolls out the awning to shade one of the benches. The beer he brings is warm, in a can that fits the man's hand like another hand, pledging friendship. He gulps the bitter water. From mouth to feet he is dry caverns, empty gullies, rocks bleached to brittle shells. He waters them all. He orders more, and more clouds empty themselves in him. The awning's narrow shade slides down the bench as the sun rolls under the sky's weight; he follows it, and finds each new inch of bench hot to the touch. The town shimmers, the heat is a spirit about to take shape. Down the empty road he sees the white house where his lover and money and clothes are. He squints at it, ready to start an argument, and it doesn't answer. He drinks and drinks and can't keep ahead of his thirst. Once or twice an hour he goes to empty his bladder behind the trailer. All is quiet, no one sees, the dirt sucks the water.

Toward evening men appear one by one in the dusk, like candles winking on, scattered over the benches and speaking low. They keep surprising him when he turns his head—why so many? But they must have colder beer. He turns to his neighbor on the bench and discovers Jackrabbit next to him.

"Looking for a drink?" asks Jackrabbit in his pinched voice.

"No," says the man, and pulls back, "don't talk to me. Don't tell me that we talk the same."

But he can't talk like anyone. He feels his tongue dead in his mouth, slurring. Jackrabbit folds his arms into his plaid shirt and waits, as if understanding that the man has already passed the point of silence, that the daylight hours have packed him full with unspoken words.

"Do you remember the volcanoes?" he asks at last.

"Volcanoes," says Jackrabbit. In his mouth the word loses its beauty. But it doesn't matter, the man is already telling everything and telling it badly, out of order, his green home, the family he left, the woman and her mother in town. Jackrabbit listens to everything, and at last says that he had a wife and child too. They were with him ten years ago, when he crossed the border.

"You have a family? Where are they?"

"God takes away," says Jackrabbit. "They were with me ten years ago."

What everyone told him was not to cross with his family. They could have told him to leave his arms behind. There were many borders and each took longer than he'd planned, each cost more money than he'd planned; but they were never robbed outright, never stranded, and after each safe crossing it seemed that his wife and child had become still deeper parts of him. His beating heart seemed to cover them all, or else his heart was a boat into which they were packed and which he steered as he steered their lives. At the last border, the desert border, they climbed with twenty others into the back of a van and bumped and swerved for hours through the dark, wreathed in heat and the smell of one another's skin. Then the small space pitched, the doors were thrown open and they were told to get out. Hands reached for them. They were brought into dry air and darkness. The earth's four directions stretched out in black and the sky hung a colder black above them. The stars had never seemed brighter or farther away.

They walked all night, facing a faint yellow bloom that was supposed to be city lights. It never came closer, its glow never cleared. Dry air rasped in their chests, the black turned slate gray and then dun, God's eye broke from the horizon and stunned them with its glory. In sidelong rays it roared: you don't know how small you are, measure yourself against this earth. The party of walkers stretched far ahead into the white sand on the horizon. The guide was already lost to sight, but others were still visible as bobbing specks crowned with black hair or pale hats; now and then the blip of a face would appear as one of them looked back at Jackrabbit and his wife. No one was behind them. Jackrabbit's wife panted and walked with shuffling steps, bent at the knees and hardly moving her hips. Her head hung slack from her shoulders. Jackrabbit took the child from her arms but they couldn't seem to walk any faster, and as the heat mounted the figures ahead winked out, one by one, against the far white. Before they vanished he saw them waving to the left, and he understood: there was a road, a police truck might come, they should wait to be picked up and taken back over the border. With his free hand he touched his wife's shoulder and guided them away from the sand, toward the embankment of mesquite and reddish dirt that dropped to the road.

They stumbled down. His right boot had split its sole and the sock was worn to netting. At each step he felt the earth grind his blisters. Their food was finished and they had only a plastic jug of turbid water that he was afraid to drink. They had filled it the previous day from a cow pond slimed over with green. His wife had taken a long drink there, she had been thirstier. Now her dry lips were parted, her breath came light and fast, and something in her look had changed; her eyes were out of light. The child, who had also drunk from the pond, twisted in Jackrabbit's hot arms.

Was it the heat of fever, was it a universal heat? His own breath burnt his nostrils. There was a fire in all things and someone's hand was slowly turning a knob, raising the flame. The road shrugged away under its cover of gray dust and cried no, too bright, you and I alike have caught fever, stay back or we'll scorch each other. There was no shade. Jackrabbit hung his shirt over a thorned branch and his wife and child lay in the scant grass beneath. No one had spoken in hours, there were no hours. The stream of time, dammed up and boiling, rose in blocks of still vapor. The sky had no forward or back, it circled light and more light, Jackrabbit's mind moved in the circle as a black dot, two black dots. They spread black wings on high. And all was held in the distant rim of mountains, the whisper of blue ridge that bled into the sky under a dark line. If he shut his eyes he would fall into the dark line and not wake.

The spirit of the desert came to him. Its bones were rock and its flesh was the sun.

I thirst, it said.

Go on, said Jackrabbit, there's nothing here for you.

There is blood, it said. I thirst.

That blood is mine. We three have mingled it. Go on.

It's not true.

Not true how? We are one flesh. I steer them under my heart.

You know it's not true. You can walk and they can't. If you stood and walked, they would remain here.

Walk where?

You saw the city lights. There are houses past those mountains. There are green lawns, shade and water.

And if they remained here?

Red salt and sweet. I thirst.

I'd come back for them. I'd find a car, a truck. They gave me a tele-phone number to call.

I thirst.

The police wouldn't find me. I would tell them there were people in the desert. They'd bring a helicopter, I would guide it.

If you leave you won't come back.

That isn't true.

You won't come back. You can walk and they can't. See the miles between you and the mountains! The light on the thorns! How many sparks of life will you bring out of the desert?

All! cried Jackrabbit. All or none! He shut his eyes and bent his body over his wife and child: he wiped out the sky, blotted the mountains from horizon to horizon, and felt wind at his brow.

In the cantina's evening all is black past the floodlights. The man's head is clearing; the beer has left a sour stain in his mouth, and now he craves warm food and water. He keeps looking to the place across the street where the women used to gather, trying to make out shapes, as if he could pick out a form that has become part of him. Jackrabbit sits as before, sloping shoulders under a thin neck.

"What happened?" asks the man.

There was a weight in the wind, a scent that reminded Jackrabbit of home. He hadn't felt it since the journey began. It pressed like a hand against his brow, relented and pressed again. When he opened his eyes he saw the dark line spread over a third of the sky, piled in gray heaps with wisped edges, and its shadow approaching fast on the scrubby plain. When it reached the sun its light went suddenly orange, then vanished, and Jackrabbit felt as if steam were lifting from him, as if he had been pulled from a hearth. Thin lightning glittered over the peaks and thunder tumbled back and forth on the plain. He uncapped the jug and dumped the foul water into the dirt, his wife opened her eyes in the gray light, raindrops struck their faces. He lifted the jug to heaven and it rattled as if filling with pebbles. An inch of clear water splashed at the bottom, he brought it down and his wife lifted the child to drink. She drank. He drank. They filled the jug with mouthfuls of water until their stomachs began to hurt, then Jackrabbit laid it down and they drew near one another in soaked clothes. Their hair plastered their faces, gray wash covered the land. It was dim as evening. They felt a chill in the water; they hadn't been cold in weeks, they had forgotten what it was like. A tremor took their shoulders. They drew closer and waited for what was coming.

XRONOS

For instance: the steering wheel bucks under your hand, refusing you, and the road starts to whip like a ribbon in the wind. The screaming animal in you looks out through the wide windscreen at a movie you've never seen, though you've been told about it since childhood: really, this? The steering wheel bucks under your hand. Like this? So strange to see the road whip, to feel the car's new drift; but stranger than the new movie is that the old movie is over. The screaming animal looks out through the windscreen. You held a hundred threads in your hand, spring was wet and summer was to be dry, Friday was cruel and Saturday was to soothe you. The road starts to whip like a ribbon in the wind. The hundred threads are out of your hand. The staircase you half climbed spins into air above you; no one will ever know half of what was in your head. Really, like this? So strange to feel the car's new drift. All you lived was prologue, the curtain hadn't lifted. The screaming animal looks out through the windscreen, dropped into a movie you've never seen. You held a hundred threads in your hand, and the road starts to whip like a ribbon in the wind. Really? Spring was wet, the staircase spins into air. The steering wheel bucks under your hand. You were told about it since childhood. Like this? The old movie? All you lived was prologue. Summer and Friday, the wide screen. Halves and threads. Threads.

CPSIA information can be obtained at www.ICGtesting.com
Printed in the USA
BVOW031056031111

274917BV00005B/1/P

9 780615 49298